DRY-GULCHE~~D~~

He landed on his feet, right hand fisting the
Colt's Frontier clear of the holster in a single
flow of movement that dragged back the
hammer and took up the trigger slack as he
lined the muzzle on Juan's chest.
Trigger loosed hammer. Hammer fell on
chamber. Fulminate erupted, igniting powder.
And the powder exploded into the confines of
the chamber, hurling raw power against the nub
of the lead slug so that it was hurled down
the grooved barrel of the gun, collecting
velocity as it spun round and round until it
reached the end and thrust out into the air on
a clean, straight line that ceased at the centre
of Juan's chest.

BREED:
Bad Habits

JAMES A. MUIR

SPHERE BOOKS LIMITED
30–32 Gray's Inn Road, London WC1X 8JL

First published by Sphere Books Ltd 1981
Copyright © James A. Muir 1981

Set in Intertype Baskerville

Printed and bound in Great Britain by
Cox & Wyman Ltd, Reading

For George, in thanks.

CHAPTER ONE

The sounds of death brought the rider to a halt. They were very distinct in the late September air, magnified by the shallow bowl of hills leading down to the Rio Grande, so that they carried clear and sharp to his position. There was the crackle of rifle fire and the duller booming of handguns, the screams of men and horses, the wetter sound of heavy blades striking soft flesh. He reined in, tilting his head to ascertain the exact position, then urged the big grey horse forwards to where the trail devolved into a shallow pass.

He dismounted there and went forwards on foot, a Winchester rifle held loose in his right hand. He was a tall man, leanly muscled and light on his feet, moving silently to the egress of the pass. He wore a wide-brimmed Sonoran stetson that shadowed his face, though had it been visible a watcher might have seen wide cheeks and a broad, strong nose above a mouth that was both sensuous and cruel. The watcher might have taken it for an Apache face, save for the piercing blue eyes and the tangled mane of shoulder-length, sun-bleached hair falling from under the hat. He wore a shirt that had once been white and was now of no particular colour, and buckskin pants tucked into knee-high, Chiracahua moccasins. Around his waist there was a gunbelt, better kept than his clothes, that held a Colt's .45 Frontier model in the holster and a wide-bladed Bowie knife in a polished sheath. Protruding from the cuff of his right moccasin there was the hilt of a slender-bladed throwing knife.

His name was Matthew Gunn.

Or Azul.

Or Breed.

It depended on who called him, and where they knew him from. He was half white, half Chiricahua Apache; and all killer. The white name was the gift of his father,

Kieron Gunn, formally given in the great cathedral at Santa Fe. Azul – the Apache name – came from his childhood in the *rancherias* of his mother's people. For Rainbow Hair was a descendant of the great war leader, Mangas Colorado, and her blue-eyed son had been named accordingly by the warriors with whom he had grown to manhood.

Breed was what they called him along the Border. And most men said it spelled Death.

He eased up to the head of the pass and stretched flat on a patch of sun-washed sand, inside the shade of a big, overhanging boulder. Beyond the rock the trail angled down in a gentle slope to a spread of pale sand bordering the river. A few clumps of mesquite protruded from the flat, interspersed with the bleached limbs of flood-strewn timber.

And bodies.

There were upwards of thirty men spread across the sand, evenly divided between the blue of United States Cavalry men and the brighter outfits of Mexican *pistole-ros*. The Cavalry men were down in a defensive circle, firing single-shot Springfield carbines at the faster-action Winchesters carried by the Mexicans. They were losing : the Mexicans were grouped back against the ridge, using their superior fire-power to cut down the troopers. Every so often one would rush forward, on foot or horseback, to slash a machete against a wounded soldier or a dying horse.

Beyond the morbid scene, the Rio Grande splashed gently blue over the shallows, only the southern edge of the river tinged with the red of men's dying.

The man called Breed watched without moving : it was not his fight, nor did he feel any particular sympathy for either side. His parents had died as a result of the bounty offered by Mexico on Apache scalps, and the Army of the United States of America had condoned that bounty.

He watched.

Watched as the blue-shirted soldiers were picked off one by one until only a single officer and a trooper remained.

Then the officer went down with a bullet plucking out

his right eye so that bits of his brain sprayed out from the back of his skull, and the trooper emptied his pistol and hurled it uselessly at the too-distant Mexicans. He was stooping to clutch another gun when a volley of rifle fire hit him and lifted him off his feet, spinning him over and over with blood spurting from the multiple holes in his body until he reached the river's edge and fell into the water. All around him, the Rio Grande got bright red, then pink as the sluggish current carried the blood away.

The Mexicans came down and began to loot the corpses. They ignored the single-shot carbines, but took all the handguns and ammunition, and whatever horses were still alive.

Azul eased back down the slope while they were still loading their spoils. Clapping one hand over the muzzle of the grey stallion, he walked the horse down the trail to a gulley and backed the animal inside. He held the stallion quiet as the Mexicans rode by, galloping fast and shouting to one another in triumph.

When they were gone he came out of his hiding place and rode down to the river. Vultures were wheeling above the carnage, and from the edge of the rocks long columns of ants were working busily towards the bodies. He rode past them, splashing into the river and fording over on the American side into Texas.

A day later he reached a town called Ysabel.

It was a one-street cow town, notable for nothing except its air of desolation. It had a saloon and an eatery, a livery stable, a bank, and a marshal's office; a few stores in between. Most of the windows were boarded over, and two buildings were burned out, the charred timbers still smouldering in the afternoon sun.

Azul went to the livery and checked his horse into a stall, then he went down the sidewalk to the marshal's office. There was a lingering odour of gunfire in the small room and a tall man with long moustaches drooping either side of his thin lips cleaning a Henry carbine.

He looked up as the halfbreed came in.

'Yeah?'

3

Azul dropped his saddlebags on a swayback chair and retained the Winchester in his folded arms.

'Saw something you might need to know. Day back, over the river.'

The tall man sniffed and set the Henry on the desk. He looked tired. He shrugged.

'Detachment of Cavalry,' said Azul, 'got wiped out by Mexicans.'

'Christ!' The peace officer's face got pale under the tan. 'That'd be Donaghue's patrol. What happened?'

'I came up late,' answered the halfbreed. 'The Mexicans had most of the horses killed and then they killed the troopers. There was about fifteen Mexicans. They went south.'

'Christ!' said the marshal for the second time. 'I gotta let Vickers know.'

He motioned for Azul to stay as he crossed the office and stuck his head out the door. A shout brought a deputy, and a muttered conversation sent the deputy down the street at a trot.

A few minutes later an Army officer came into the room.

He had the chevrons of a major on his coat, and under the neatly-trimmed beard that covered most of his lower face his lips were tense.

'Tell me,' he said.

Azul told him.

The Army man looked at the marshal, then at Azul.

'They went south?'

The halfbreed nodded, not speaking.

'About fifteen of them?'

Azul nodded again.

'You didn't go after them?'

Azul shook his head. 'Why should I?'

The Army man looked him up and down. Then:

'Forgive me, I should introduce myself: Ben Vickers. Major in the United States Cavalry. In command of this stretch of the Border. This is,' he pointed at the lawman, 'Marshal Jeff Howe. You are?'

He left the question hanging.

'Matthew Gunn,' said Azul.

4

'I know that name.' Howe's voice was harsh suddenly. 'I read it. Wait!'

He tugged a drawer open and began to rummage through a mess of papers. After a while he said, 'Christ! Yes: you're called Breed, ain't you?'

Azul nodded, letting the Winchester slide down his arm so that the muzzle angled midway between the peace officer and the Cavalryman.

'You're lucky,' said Howe. 'You ain't wanted here, else I'd hafta to take you in.'

'Maybe,' said Azul.

'Forget it,' said Vickers in a parade ground voice that cut through the animosity in Howe's tone. 'He could be useful to me.'

He turned to face Azul, a smile coming out from behind the beard, 'I'd like to buy you a drink, mister Gunn.'

Azul shrugged and Howe glared.

'Fine. Let's go.'

They went out of the marshal's office and down the street to a saloon called *The Lucky Cow*.

The frontage was pocked with bullet holes and one of the big windows flanking the batwings was covered with recently-nailed planks. Inside the air was warm and smoky, more bullet holes showing in the walls, on a line with the door and the shattered window. A handful of men were bellied up against the bar or seated at the small tables scattered the length of the low-ceilinged room. There were two haggard women in frayed silk dresses and darned stockings encouraging the drinkers to part with their money. A barkeep with a fringe of mouse-brown hair ringing his glistening skull looked up as they approached.

'Whisky,' said Vickers. 'The good stuff.'

The man stooped to fetch a bottle from under the counter. Unlike the others shelved behind him, it had a label. He filled two glasses and left the bottle standing between them. Vickers raised his in a kind of toast.

'Might be I got a proposition for you.'

Azul swallowed whisky, not speaking; waiting for the Army man to continue.

5

'What the marshal said was true.' It was impossible to tell whether it was a question or a statement, and he continued without awaiting a reply. 'Matthew Gunn, otherwise known as Azul. Sometimes called Breed. You've got quite a reputation, mister Gunn. You're lucky there's no dodger on you in this county, or Jeff Howe'd have you locked up an' waiting for the prison wagon.'

'Maybe,' murmured Azul. 'Maybe not.'

Vickers ignored the implication. 'You're half Apache and you know the territory. Both sides of the river.' Vickers poured more liquor. 'You're fast with a gun and you can track good as any scout. I could use you.'

'For what?' asked the halfbreed. 'I'm just passing through.'

'Listen.' Vickers sipped his drink, his grey eyes thoughtful. 'For around four months now this area's been raided by Mexican bandits. They seem to know when there's money around, and where it is. San Jacinto, Placerville, El Paso, Ysabel, they've hit them all. The banks have changed their delivery schedules and the stageline's altered its times and its routes. It don't make no difference : the bandits still take the money. They come in fast and they go faster. They've escaped every patrol I've sent after them, and once they cross the border my men are lost.'

'There's a Ranger station at El Paso,' said Azul. 'What about them?'

'The Texas Rangers have sent men after them, too,' replied Vickers. 'But the Mexes always lose them in the hills. The Jornados.'

'That's rough country,' murmured Azul.

'Yeah.' Vickers nodded. 'That's why I figgered to trap them this side of the Rio Grande. I got word they hit Placerville a week back. Figgered Ysabel would be next, so I sent Lieutenant Donaghue to wait up on the river. That was the fight you saw. It sounds like they knew Donaghue'd be waiting for them. Anyway, they hit town all right. Come straight in like a regular cavalry charge, shooting up the town and hitting the bank. They got away with close on fifteen thousand dollars. Add what they took outta Placerville and El Paso, and you've got

6

around forty thousand in coin and paper.'

Azul shook his head. 'That much takes some carrying. The men I saw were riding light.'

'That's the crazy thing.' Vickers nodded, looking worried. 'The amounts they been taking, they'd need a wagon – pack horses, at least – to get it all clear, but they go out fast as they come in.'

'Maybe they cache it,' suggested Azul. 'Or there's a wagon pick-up fixed.'

It was Vickers' turn to shake his head. 'I've had patrols turn over every goddam possible hiding place in three days' ride : there's nowhere. Nor any sign of them transferring to wagons. It just disappears, like the goddam bandits.'

'So?' Azul shrugged, and accepted a fresh drink. 'What's it got to do with me?'

'You're a tracker.' Vicker's tone was earnest now, and his grey eyes fastened intently on the halfbreed's face. 'And you can cross the border. I want you to wait around and follow them. Find out where they go. What the hell they do with the money. One man – you – could do that.'

'They have to get it into Mexico somehow,' said Azul, softly. 'Knowing where they go won't help you : the Army can't cross the line.'

'The hell we can't,' snapped Vickers. 'You find out where they're going and I'll have a detachment backed up with Rangers go in after them. And screw the regulations.'

'Maybe,' said Azul. 'But there's one problem.'

'What?' the major asked.

'I'm not interested.' Azul emptied his glass and set it down on the bar. I'm no hired scout, and I don't owe Ysabel or El Paso a thing. Like I said : I'm just passing through. So thanks for the drink, but no thanks.'

Vickers' face creased in an angry frown and he tugged at his beard. 'You just saw sixteen good cavalrymen slaughtered. Don't that mean anything to you?'

Azul shrugged. 'I've seen *good cavalrymen* slaughter Apache women. That meant something to me.'

'Jesus!' grunted Vickers. 'I'll pay you. Regular scout's wage.'

'Give it to a regular scout,' said Azul. 'I'm not interested.'

'What they say about you's true.' Vickers' voice was harsh now, rising as the anger took hold. 'You're just a goddam killer.'

'But not wanted here,' Azul reminded him. 'Goodbye, Major.'

He fetched a coin from his vest and dropped it on the bar. 'For the drinks.'

Vickers watched as he turned away, swinging his saddlebags over his left shoulder and canting the Winchester against his right. The major emptied his own glass and stamped out of the saloon. Azul watched him go, then beckoned the barkeep over.

'You got anywhere I can sleep? And get a bath?'

The bald man looked at him with red-tinged eyes and shook his head.

'Not fer a goddam halfbreed that don't give a damn about them fine sojer boys gettin' killed I don't. An' don't try to buy no more drinks here. I ain't servin' you.'

Azul shrugged and walked towards the batwings. Behind him, he heard the barkeep talking loudly to the listening men.

He went out of the saloon and crossed the street. It was busier now, work teams clearing the wreckage of the two burned-out houses and store-keepers re-arranging their windows. He went to the stable and asked the same old man who had checked the grey stallion in if he could use the water trough, and sleep in the loft. The old man agreed; for three dollars. Azul went out back and stripped down, sluicing under the pump and rubbing his body with sand. Then he dried himself on his blanket and went back inside the stable.

The old man met him at the stall containing the grey horse.

'I took yore money,' he said, 'so you can stay over like we agreed. But that's the last of it. You be gone come mornin'.'

Azul nodded, accepting the inevitable. Then, as an afterthought, 'How many folks from town went after the Mexicans?'

The old man looked confused. 'How many? None. What we got the Army for? An' the Rangers?'

'Yeah,' said the halfbreed. 'What?'

'Don't make no diff'rence,' grumbled the oldster. 'You ain't welcome here. I heard what you told the Major from Billy Angstrom.'

'Who's he?' asked Azul.

'You'll find out soon enough.' The old man dug a finger into his right nostril and flicked the pokings onto the straw. 'Ain't fer me to say. But were I you, I'd get gone now.'

'You want to give me my money back?' Azul asked.

The old man shook his head. 'We made a deal, feller. I'll stick by that. What you stick by, that's yore problem.'

He picked up a broom and began to sweep out the aisle with a concentration that excluded any further talk. Azul stowed his saddlebags and rifle inside the stall and went out onto the street. He was hungry.

He crossed the street to the eatery. It was early evening, a big yellow moon already showing in the sky, looking waxy against the fading blue. It didn't seem like word had reached the owners of the restaurant yet, because he was given a table and asked what he wanted. He ordered steak and hash browns, with collard greens on the side. A pot of coffee. In the morning, he decided, he would ride north and west, back into New Mexico, taking his time to drift up into the Mogallons. His mother's people would be starting the movement south – those not already hiding in Mexico, or settled on reservations – and he would go back to the place where his parents had died. It had been a long time.

He finished his meal and settled the bill. The woman who took his money was thin and grey-haired. She had worried eyes that got frightened as she told him he couldn't eat breakfast there.

'It ain't me,' she said. 'I don't give a damn who I serve. But if you come back, I ain't gonna get no more custom in this town. Billy said so.'

'Billy?' asked Breed.

'Bill Angstrom,' said the woman, looking surprised that he didn't know the name, and repeating it to be sure,

'Billy Angstrom.'

'Fine.' Azul stood up. 'Who is he?'

The woman gulped and began to brush at her bun of faded hair. 'Just get out, will you? Please.'

Azul got out.

The street was dark now, the sun gone down over the horizon and the moon lifted up high enough that it filled Ysabel with pale yellow light. The air was still warm, a slight breeze blowing from the south so that the tumbleweeds shifted nervously over the packed dirt. A black and white dog scratched itself vigorously at the centre of the street, yawned, and slunk away under the sidewalk. A light glowed from the marshal's office, another from *The Lucky Cow*. The rest of Ysabel was in darkness.

Azul looked across mainstreet to the single small lantern burning above the door of the stable. He felt filled and sleepy, pleased to be sleeping the night on hay, with the familiar smell of horses around him, rather than in a bug-ridden bed inside a dirty room. He stepped down off the sidewalk.

And a voice said, 'Hold it, feller!'

Instantly he was awake. The voice had come from the porch to his left, from slightly behind him. It was threatening, but not dangerous: had the speaker wished simply to kill him, he would have fired first and spoken after. As it was, he had Azul's back covered – if his gun was drawn – but the halfbreed was turned sideways on, his gunhand hidden by his body. Instinct settled his right hand close to the butt of the Colt's Frontier as he froze.

He waited, knowing he had a chance.

'Turn around.' The voice sounded young, pitched up into hardness by whisky and bravado. 'I want to see yore face.'

He turned, and saw a man of around twenty-one, wearing black leather pants and a matching vest. A gunbelt hung too low on his waist, and a wide-brimmed stetson pulled too tight over his eyes. He had black hair and a carefully-combed moustache. The teeth were very white as he grinned.

'So you're Breed. I hear you're good. With a gun, I mean. Otherwise I hear you're just a dirty, no-account spillin' off a squawman.'

Cold rage filled Azul's mind, and his immediate instinct was to draw his gun and kill the man for the insult to his parents. But training won out. There were two other men leaning against the poles of the sidewalk, passing a bottle between them. And he remembered something his father had told him . . .

You'll get insults thrown at you for what you are. Don't let them get to you. You let that happen, and you lose the edge. You got nothin' to be ashamed of. Remember that.

And the words of old Sees-The-Fox: *Rage is a fine madness but it must be chanelled. Let anger control you, and you become stupid. Control it; direct it; let it work for you. Against your enemy, so that his rage destroys him, while yours keeps you alive to fight again.*

'What do you want?' he asked, facing the man. 'Who are you?'

'Name's Billy Angstrom. I want to kill you.'

'Why?' asked Azul.

Angstrom laughed. A high-pitched sound, almost hysterical. 'Because you're a goddam dirty halfbreed that don't want to know about the bandits.'

Azul let his eyes flicker towards the two men on the sidewalk. They had dropped the bottle now, and both were standing with hands thumbed casually into their belts. Close to their guns. More people were spilling out of the saloon, and others from the surrounding buildings. No-one looked friendly. He decided that if he killed Billy he would be shot down soon after.

'I'll not draw on you,' he said. 'There's no point.'

'The hell there's no point,' snarled Billy. 'Draw, you bastard!'

Azul shook his head and stepped forwards, keeping his hands well clear of his waist. Billy dropped to a crouch, knees bent and right arm hooked over his gun. Like he thought gunfighters stood.

'Draw, you squaw bastard! Or I'll kill you where you stand!'

Azul wasn't standing anymore. Instead he was coming

forwards in three easy paces that brought him within range of Billy Angstrom's body as he launched himself into the air and powered both feet against Billy's chest.

The move took the would-be gunfighter by surprise. He cannoned back with his hand lurching clear of his pistol. Spread his length in the moonlit dust and gasped as he hit the ground. He spat and began to fist the Colt from the holster. Azul rolled over, lifting to his knees and diving forwards to slap his left hand over Billy's wrist as his right came down to bounce across the mouth. Billy spat blood and caught hold of Azul's hand. The half-breed ground a knee down hard against the right arm and punched Billy in the stomach. Billy gagged, then tried to drive his knees against Azul's back. The half-breed ignored the kicking as he reached over to take the Colt from Billy's hand and toss it onto the sidewalk. Then he shifted clear of the body and lifted to his feet, bringing Billy with him. He came upright with his left hand fastened on Billy's shirt. His right splayed open, slapping back and forth over the young man's face.

He held him like that for a minute or more, just holding Billy upright as his open hand spread bruises over the youth's cheeks and Billy's head rocked like a clock's pendulum, right to left and back again, until blood spilled from the lips and Billy's eyes got glazed over.

No-one spoke until Azul let the boy go. Then there was a sigh from the crowd, like the ending of a sermon in church as Billy crumpled back on his heels and fell full length into the dirt.

Azul watched him fall, then turned away. The crowd parted as he walked towards the stable, not speaking, just watching him go with lowered eyes and unspoken comments.

He was at the doors before a word was said.

And that came from Billy Angstrom. A single word, 'Bastard!'

Azul spun round as he heard it. It was accompanied by the familiar sound of a pistol's hammer clicking back. The sound of *tense, half-cock,* and *ready.*

He drew as he heard it all. Dropped on his side with

his own gun lifting from the holster with the hammer snapping back as his forefinger closed on the slack of the trigger and his thumb let go the hammer.

Flame blasted from across the street, and he sensed, rather than heard, the whistle of a bullet over his head. His own gun bucked once in his hand and there was a scream. Then he fired again : *Once is dead, twice is safe.*

The first bullet hit Billy Angstrom in the chest. It tore through his shirt and the flesh beneath to score a furrow of blood down his torso, tunnelling into his body just over his belt. It continued to plough on through the muscle of his belly until it lodged against his pelvic girdle, just over his testicles. The nervous shock jerked him upright with a high-pitched scream erupting from his mouth as he dropped his gun and fastened both hands tight around the core of his manhood. So he was lifted up for the second, which punctured his stomach and ricochetted off the splinters of bone already draining his life away into his left lung. His screaming ended on a huge gout of blood that fountained from his mouth and sprayed onto the dirt of the street. It splattered over the sand, coloured black in the moon's light, puddling dark around Billy's body as he closed his mouth and his eyes and pitched forwards into the dark pit of death.

Azul stood up.

There was a silence.

Then someone said, 'Goddam halfbreed.'

And someone else said, 'Killer.'

And Marshal Howe came through the crowd with a sawed-down Remington shotgun in his hands, and said, 'All right. What's going on?'

'Billy Angstrom's dead,' said someone. 'The half-breed killed him.'

'Yeah!' The crowd took up the call, like a wolfpack. 'It was the Breed. He beat up on Billy, then he shot him.'

Howe angled the shotgun in Azul's direction and cocked both hammers.

'I guess you're livin' up to yore reputation,' he said. 'Drop the gun, an' come forwards with yore hands in the air.'

Then a voice that was soft and quiet – and all the

more forceful for its certitude – said, 'It was a fair fight, marshal. The young man tried to shoot the other man in the back.'

Azul and the marshal and the crowd gaped together at the woman who had spoken. She was tall – close on five feet six or seven – and dressed in black. The breeze flattened her robe against the contours of her body so that Azul got the impression of long legs and firm breasts, a trim, flat waist. A kind of hood obscured her hair, banded at the front by a strip of white that framed an oval face with big dark eyes and a full mouth. The half-breed realised with surprise that she was a nun.

'Best you stay outta this, Sister,' said Howe, sounding confused. 'It ain't yore business.'

'The sanctity of life is my business, marshal.' The answer was said in the same soft, firm voice. 'I saw it all, and I can give you my word that the young man was trying to shoot the other gentleman in the back.'

'That's right.' A second black-clad figure stepped forwards. 'We saw it all.'

'It was attempted murder,' said a third nun. Pointing at Azul as she added, 'He was just defending himself.'

'Christ!' said Howe.

And Azul grinned and said, 'I guess I got the angels on my side.'

CHAPTER TWO

'Look,' Marshal Howe ran a hand through his hair and stared at the three nuns. 'You're makin' this difficult for me.'

'The truth is seldom easy,' murmured the tallest. 'Nor following its way.'

In the glow of the kerosene lantern hanging from the peace officer's ceiling Azul could see that his first impression of the woman had been correct. She was beautiful. He wondered what her body looked like. Wondered if it matched the perfect configuration of eyes and nose and mouth. Wondered what colour her hair might be.

He glanced at the others. One was short and plump, with a pale face and wide blue eyes above a snub nose and a rosebud mouth. The third was Mexican-looking, with coal-dark eyes and sensuous lips that would have graced a high-class whore. He wondered why they had chosen to take up the veil.

'I still got a town full of people ready to lynch him,' grumbled Howe. 'I take yore word he killed Billy fair, but that don't alter the fact that folks round here knew Billy. Liked him.'

'That hardly justifies giving an innocent man to a lynch mob,' said the first nun. 'Does it?'

'Christ Jesus!' spluttered Howe, then shrugged an apology. 'Beggin' yore pardon, sister, but I wasn't plannin' that.'

'What were you planning, marshal?' The nun's voice was cool.

'Oh, hell!' Howe was getting embarrassed. 'I was goin' to jail him until the circuit court come round. That was all.'

'And fight off your friends out there?' The nun indicated the street with a sideways glance. 'For how long?'

'What's it matter to you?' Howe asked, defensively.

'Life is sacred,' she replied. 'Our Lord witnesses the fall of the tiniest sparrow.'

'He ain't no goddam sparrow,' snarled Howe. 'He's a halfbreed with a reputation for killing.'

'Judge not, lest ye be judged,' said the pale-faced nun

The marshal slapped both hands on the desk and shook his head wearily. 'All right. What you suggest? I'll agree he killed Billy fair, but you want me to turn him loose? He wouldn't get across the street.'

At the window, a deputy turned to say, 'More comin', Jeff. Close on fifty out there now.'

'How'd they look?' asked the lawman.

'Angry,' said the deputy. 'They got a rope.'

As though to emphasise his point, a stone rattled off the bars covering the right-side window, and a voice started a chant that was taken up by the mob.

'Bring him out. Hang him high.'

'Look,' said Howe, 'I got one deputy an' fifty people out there already. There's two hundred live in this town, all of them knowin' Billy Angstrom. His poppa runs the hardware store, an' gives good credit. Come mornin' they'll all be shoutin' for the halfbreed's neck. What the hell you want me to do?'

'Your duty,' said the tallest nun. 'What else?'

'Christ!' mumbled the peace officer. 'My duty's to this town. I can throw him in jail an' hope they wait for the circuit judge to come round, or I can give him to them now.'

'There is another way,' said the nun.

'What way?' asked Howe. 'I don't see no other way.'

'We had planned to leave tomorrow,' said the nun. 'To start back for our convent. We could take him with us. A guide would be useful.'

Howe shrugged. 'Sister, if you could do that I'd be grateful. But how?'

'We have a wagon,' said the nun. 'We could bring it to the rear of your jail and take mister Gunn on board. Then leave tonight.'

'All right,' said Howe. 'That makes sense to me.'

Azul spoke for the first time, 'I got a horse in the stable. I'm not leaving it.'

The tall nun turned to her companions: 'Fetch the horse. Hitch it to the wagon team.'

Then, to Azul, 'What does it look like?'

Azul described the grey stallion, and added that his saddlebags and rifle were in the stall. The tall nun nodded and gestured for the others to go. Howe showed them out the back door of the jail, leaving Azul and the other nun alone with the deputy.

The halfbreed was surprised by the determination of the three holy women, and asked the sister why she was taking this much trouble.

'I see no reason for a man to be killed,' she said. 'You were innocent of any crime, yet you would have been hung had I not intervened.'

Azul nodded, acknowledging his debt; and asked her name.

'I am Sister Teresa,' she replied. 'Sister Julia and Sister Maria are fetching the wagon. If you take us to the convent, we shall pay you one hundred dollars.'

'Where?' asked the halfbreed.

'Santa Rosa,' said the nun. 'Our convent is there.'

'Mexico,' said Azul. 'In the Jornados.'

'Bandit country,' Sister Teresa nodded. 'That is why we need an escort.'

Azul started to say something, but a fresh rattle of stones against the window persuaded him it was better to keep his mouth closed and go along with the nuns.

'The wagon's here,' said Howe. 'Let's go.'

He opened the door at the rear of the jail and checked the alley beyond. It was empty, save for the big wagon with a four-horse team up front and the two nuns on the drive seat, and Azul's horse tethered behind. He waved Azul and Sister Teresa down the unlit corridor fronting the cells.

The alley was dark. Darker once Howe slammed the door shut. Azul helped Teresa into the wagon and fetched his horse up to the front. He mounted and steered down the alley as the sound of shouting got louder behind him.

They went out of Ysabel to the east, skirting round

the backyards and little vegetable plots of the town until they were onto the flat beyond and riding hard to circle over to the south. The moon was up high now, lighting the plain near bright as day, and from behind them there came the echo of raised voices and stamping feet. Azul fell back behind the wagon, watching their back trail until he was sure there was no vigilante posse coming after them, then reined in.

It was sometime after midnight. The moon was fading over in the east and a slow light was beginning to brighten the distant horizon. Mist was starting to rise from the country around and ahead of them, lifting up in pale, wraith-like shapes from the ground before joining together to form an ethereal mist that hung a few feet clear of the trail before joining into a solid fog of damp, grey air that obscured vision and left their clothes wet with the clinging globules of water.

They halted on Azul's command where a ravine split their forwards passage, and turned the wagon into the split of cut ground to where an overhang hid them and gave shelter.

Whatever primeval force had burst the ground had left an overhang of wind-washed stone above a kind of balcony that was wide enough to take the wagon and hide it beneath the lip of rock.

Sister Teresa steered in with an expertise that surprised Azul.

She parked the wagon and climbed down in a swirl of petticoats that exposed a trim white thigh that had nothing at all to do with a nun. Azul helped the other sisters to the ground and went to feed the horses.

By the time he came back they had food cooking.

'Why?' he asked. 'Why'd you do it?'

'What?' asked Teresa. 'I don't understand.'

'Nor do I,' said Azul. 'Why'd you argue to save me?'

'We needed you,' said the nun. 'To get us back to Santa Rosa.'

The halfbreed shrugged and ate his breakfast.

The three women showed little sign of fatigue when Azul roused them at sunrise and got the wagon moving again. The big horses settled into the traces and began to plod forwards, not fast but with a relentless steadiness that suggested they could keep up the pace all day. The wagon creaked as it lurched clear of the ravine, the bed settled hard on the springs under the weight of the tarpaulin-covered load. Azul stared at the lashed-down canvas and brought the grey stallion abreast of the drive seat.

'What you carrying?' he asked. 'That's a lot of weight in back.'

'Does it matter?' Sister Teresa smiled at him.

The halfbreed shrugged. 'It might. If there's a lynch mob comes after us.'

'I don't think they would harm us.' The woman frowned slightly. 'And you could out run them, then come back to meet us.'

'And bandits?' Azul pressed his point. 'We're riding into some rough country.'

'Would Mexicans dare attack three Brides of Christ?' It was said with a perfect confidence. 'I hardly think so.'

'Yaquis would,' grunted Azul. 'Or Apache.'

'Our very reason for wanting you along, mister Gunn.' Her calm smile dismissed the problem. 'To protect us.'

'But you could still need to run,' countered Azul. 'And you can't with that load.'

'Nor can we leave it,' replied the nun. 'It contains religious objects for our convent. They were the reason we came north. The Reverend Mother entrusted us with their delivery, and we cannot betray that trust.'

Azul shook his head in disbelief. 'You mean you've been travelling the border country for that? How come you didn't hire a guard before?'

Sister Teresa went on smiling serenely. 'Our faith has been our guard, mister Gunn. Our habit our protection. You of all people cannot deny that power : it saved your life.'

'I guess.' Azul shrugged, knowing when he was beaten. He turned the grey stallion clear of the wagon and circled back to check the trail for sign of pursuit. The country was mostly flat here, broken by occasional gulleys and ravines, but mostly a wide expanse of dry land stretching down to the Rio Grande before any real vegetation showed. The trail ahead went into a border town called simply El Rio that wasn't much more than a trading post with a store and cantina and a few houses. It was a popular crossing point for anyone not especially interested in meeting the law, for the Mexicans who ran the place asked no questions so long as a man had money. It was two days ahead, at the wagon's speed.

Azul spent the days scouting the ground in front of them and checking his back trail. He guessed that the furore in Ysabel had died down by now, and that the mob howling for his neck had dispersed back to whatever occupations normally earned the citizens their livings. A few people crossed his path, but they mostly just nodded the time of day and moved on. One was a Mexican peasant herding a laden burro down towards the river; two more were cowboys, riding line for a spread thirty miles out of Ysabel; one was a hard-faced man in a black suit that matched the colour of the big black horse he rode, who said his name was Ryker and accepted a cup of coffee before moving on.

Mostly, the days were empty, starting at sunup with the three nuns mouthing prayers, then more over their mid-day meal, and more still when they halted at night. Azul paid little attention to the devotions, preferring to spend his time checking the horses or the wagon or his guns.

And around noon on the second day they came in sight of El Rio.

The terrain was totally flat here, stretching down to the river along the length of a wide meadow where sheep grazed and low trees dotted the landscape, growing thicker as they approached the water. The town was surrounded by a circle of windoaks and willows, the buildings standing out from amongst the greenery. The houses were adobe-built, with flat roofs and wide, tile-covered porches. Only the cantina – cum-store stood higher than a single storey, its frontage further enhanced by an arch built up from the roof to carry the legend, *Cantina El Rio*. And underneath, in Mexican and American, *Next stop Mexico*.

The place was quiet as they rode in. A few dogs were stretched over the packed dirt of the street and a few old men sat in the shade, barely moving their sombreros as the wagon passed by. Azul skirted round the cantina to the corral at the rear.

Sister Teresa asked him why they were stopping.

'After this,' he replied, 'we've got about five days hard country to cross. I want the horses rested. We can stock up on supplies here, then make for Marisco. Then we go on to Santa Rosa.'

There was a muttered conversation between the three nuns before Sister Teresa nodded and said, 'All right, mister Gunn. But only for one night, we must start again at dawn.'

Azul nodded and began to rub down the grey stallion. Two Mexicans came out from the cantina and offered to handle the wagon horses. Sister Teresa promised them a dollar each, and Azul led the unlikely group into the building.

El patrón greeted them with surprise. He was not accustomed to providing rooms for *Las Religiosas*, but he would do his best. Which meant that three whores were ordered off to spend the night where they could while the sisters got a bed each. Azul opted to sleep out, close to the wagon.

'I should like to bathe,' said Sister Teresa. 'Is it possible?'

El Patrón shrugged and pointed over his shoulder. 'The river is the only place we have, *hermana*.'

'Then we shall use the river,' nodded the nun. And turned to Azul, 'Will you please come with us? In case there are any watchers.'

Azul shrugged and followed the three women out of the cantina.

The southbound trail went straight through El Rio to the bank of the river. Off to the right a shallow oxbow had carved a sandy island and an inwards curve, both thick with willows. Grass grew down to the water's edge where it curved gently into the shallow stream.

'Please stay here,' ordered Sister Teresa, 'with your back turned. If anyone comes, send them away.'

21

Azul nodded and slumped down against the trunk of a willow. It was still and quiet, the only sound the soporific drumming of the cicadas. He looked at the sky. It was very blue, partially covered with scudding white clouds that drifted lazy over the wide emptiness. The air was warm, heavy with the scent of the trees. Then, behind him, he heard the sound of splashing water and giggling. He turned, not able to resist the temptation, and peered through the willow fronds.

The three women were in the water. And they looked, now, like women rather than nuns :

Sister Teresa's body was as good as he had imagined it. Long and clean and lithe. Her breasts, the nipples erected by the chill of the river, bounced as she splashed herself, and he was surprised to see that her hair was long and nutmeg brown : he had always thought that nuns shaved their heads.

Sister Julia was equally long-haired, though in her case it was a mane of natural curls that dripped wetly about her face with a few tendrils reaching down to the fullness of her plump bosom. Her body was very white, the pubic hair matching the curls on her head.

Sister Maria was dark, her body the colour of chocolate, except where the paleness of the aureoles gave way to coffee-brown nipples, and where a dark thatch of pubic hair spread between her legs. She, too, was long-haired, straight folds of near-black wrapping in seductive curtains about her face.

It was hard to decide which looked the most attractive. Or which looked least like a nun.

Azul turned away, feeling slightly ashamed, and settled back under the willow tree.

And then a muffled scream brought him to his feet.

He came upright with the Colt's Frontier swinging clear of the holster as his thumb took the hammer back and his eyes scanned the path to the river. There were two men he recognised vaguely down in the water. One was holding Sister Teresa and the other was pointing a Remington Army model at the other nuns. The man holding Teresa was thin and dark-haired, dressed in a blue denim shirt and brown pants. He had a Colt's Peacemaker pressed up against the nun's face and his left arm was fastened tight about her body, his hand clawed over her breasts. The other man was shorter and fatter, with a freckled face and carroty hair. He was herding Julia and Maria out of the river with a big, ugly grin on his face.

Azul came down through the trees and halted inside the cover of a low-hung willow, watching and listening.

'All right,' snarled the thin man as he wrestled Teresa clear of the water. 'Where is he?'

'I don't know,' said the nun, her voice surprisingly calm. 'Please let us get dressed.'

'What for?' asked the red-head. 'No point puttin' on what you're gonna take off.'

'After we find the halfbreed, Aaron,' said the dark-haired man. 'He's first.'

'Why?' asked Sister Teresa. 'Why do you want him?'

'He killed Billy Angstrom,' said the thin man. 'An' Billy was a friend of ours. Maybe we should introduce ourselves.' He parodied a bow, still holding tight to Teresa. 'My friend up there is Aaron Grange. Me, I'm Ned Thatcher. An' we don't take kindly to squaw's spillin's killing our friends.'

Grange was backing out of the water with the Remington drifting between the two other naked women. His eyes were big and wide as he stared at their bodies. His back was to Azul.

The halfbreed lowered the Colt's hammer slow and quiet. Slid the gun back into the holster, and drew the throwing knife clear of his moccasin. He balanced the blade on the palm of his hand, thumb taking the weight of the haft. And calculated the distance.

Grange was moving slowly up the slope, feeling his way through the trees as his eyes and his gun hovered over the two women. Thatcher was holding Teresa in front of him, his left hand now fastened on her wrists as he angled the Colt up the slope.

Azul raised his arm high and swung it down in a single, clean motion that sent the knife spinning out from his hand in a whirl of glittering movement. The blade spun circles through the air that ended in Ned Thatcher's throat. It cleaved in through the hollow below the adam's apple, slicing the soft flesh like a wire cutting butter, and hit the bone of the spine beyond. Thatcher gargled a scream, triggering one shot into the air as he pitched back, dropping his gun as he tried to snatch the pain from his neck. He ground his heels into the soft earth of the riverbank as he spanned his length over the ground, both hands reaching up to pluck at the pain filling his throat and mind. His groping fingers cut on the blade, spreading a thin spill of blood over his face as he dragged it free and the flow got faster as his windpipe pulsed thick spumes of crimson out from the hole in his neck. A thin, high scream erupted from his mouth, cascading off a fountain of blood as he slid down into the Rio Grande, propelled by the twitching movement of his own feet.

Aaron Grange turned, swinging his pistol clear of the women to attempt to line it on Azul. The halfbreed shot him while he was halfway round. His hand, dropped loose of the throwing knife, was lined on the butt of his Colt. He fisted the gun from the holster and snapped off a shot that took Grange under the left arm. It went in through the ribs, piercing a lung so that a huge gout of blood fountained from the red-head's mouth. He spun round, losing his footing as he fell back down the slope. The second bullet hit his chin, shattering the bone before splintering his teeth and ploughing on through the roof of his mouth to imbed in the soft tissue of his brain. It stopped inside his skull, but by then Aaron Grange was dead, only his automatic body movements continuing to pump streams of scarlet from his mouth and nose.

Azul thumbed the spent shells clear of the Colt as the three nuns scrambled for their clothes. He reloaded on five cylinders and dropped the pistol back inside the holster. Then he went down to fetch his knife clear of Ned Thatcher's body. He wiped it clean on the man's shirt and washed it in the river. Then he went back up the slope to where the nuns were waiting.

They were dressed, looking damp and very calm as he approached them.

'They came from Ysabel,' said Sister Teresa. 'I recognised them.'

'Godless bastards,' said Sister Julia. 'They deserved to be killed.'

'Do we pray for them?' asked Sister Maria.

'I think not,' said Teresa. 'I think it might be best to leave here quickly!'

'Tomorrow,' said Azul. 'They were friends of Billy Angstrom, there won't be any more coming.'

'Now,' said the nun, 'quickly.'

Azul shrugged and escorted them back to the cantina, where they bought provisions and set out fast.

'Like the religion you follow,' he grumbled. 'You never know when the second going's coming.'

CHAPTER THREE

Over the river the ground broke up after a day into broken terrain.

The fording was easy : a shallow crossing that left most of the wagon clear of the water as it traversed the bed of the Rio Grande. Then there was a stretch of meadow land like the verdant north side. But after that, the country got rough and rocky, lifting up towards the Jornados in a series of folds that started just south of the river and got progressively higher as the journey continued. At first there was a spread of foothills that trailed ravines and dry gulches in a criss-cross pattern over their path as the land got higher and steeper, stretching away into the high-rising bulk of the main range. The trail cut up through a series of folds that became steadily harder to negotiate, at times winding along long curved paths that would suddenly descend into steep declines, at others becoming a purely vertical ascent. Their passage was slow, hampered by the weight of the wagon, and only maintained by the strength of the four big horses hauling it steadily upwards.

After a while they came out onto a high plateau where the wind blew constantly cold and buzzards circled the sky above them as if waiting for them to stop and die. The ground here was flat and arid, a great expanse of dry, rocky land that was broken only by the boulders and the odd clump of wind-washed mesquite. Beyond the spread of the plateau, the high-lifting bulks of the Jornados range was a dark promise against the skyline.

And on the fifth day they reached Marisco.

The town was spread like dry bones along the scarp of the Jornado range. The adobe houses stood out from the grey frontage of the mountains like a skeletal spread left to bleach and die on the granite walls. It was a long line of houses following a natural terrace in the mountainside, the southernmost buildings settled close up against the rocky walls, the northern buildings perched on the rim of the wide ledge with their rears almost ready to fall over the cliff. There was a single street dividing the two rows, its surface hard stone. There was a church and a stable at one end, a *federale* station and a cantina at the other. The *federale* station was boarded up, with spiders' webs strung over the planking. The church looked much the same. In between there were a few stores, none of them looking much better.

Azul led the way into the stable, where an old man crossed himself when he saw the nuns.

'*Madre de Dios*!' he muttered. 'It has been a long time since *las hermanas* came here.'

'What happened to your church?' asked Sister Teresa. 'Why is it closed?'

'*Los bandidos*,' said the old man. 'They came and killed the *padre*. They said they would kill us if we opened it again. So we didn't.'

'They will not kill us,' said the nun. 'We shall open it.'

'I wish you wouldn't,' said the old man. 'You will be gone soon, but we have to stay here.'

'Only to pray,' said the woman, calmly. 'We shall not be here long, so trust us.'

Azul watched the three nuns go down the street to the church, then turned away to tend the horses. What they did was their own affair.

'They will bring us trouble,' muttered the old man. 'That is all the Church ever brings people like us.'

Azul shrugged and went inside the cantina.

It was cool and clean. It didn't look like too many people had used it in some time, and the man behind the bar looked up with an expression of pleasure, or maybe gratitude, on his face. Azul asked for tequila, then enquired about rooms.

The barkeep shrugged and said he had a cabin out back with a big bed.

When Azul explained he wanted a place for three nuns to sleep the barkeep laughed and made an obscene gesture.

'*Hombre*,' he said, 'I don't have nowhere except the

whore's bed. They can sleep there. But otherwise it's the stable.'

Azul drank tequila and decided the stable would be better.

After a while the nuns came back, trooping into the cantina like three dark swans. The halfbreed explained the sleeping arrangements, and Sister Teresa nodded.

'We can accept hardship,' she said. 'It is no trouble.'

'I'll be in there, too,' said Azul.

The woman smiled and settled a hand on his arm. 'We trust you, mister Gunn. After all, you protected us back at El Rio.'

'Yeah,' said Azul, not sure how he could take sleeping so close to the three women after seeing them naked. 'Thanks.'

'It is our pleasure,' said Teresa. 'We are grateful to have you come with us.'

Azul nodded, and went off to find food.

They ate chili that was more beans than meat, with hard bread on the side and rancid coffee. Then they sorted out the sleeping arrangements. It was agreed that the three nuns would occupy the empty stalls at the rear of the stable, and Azul would sleep close by the front door. He slung his saddle on the hay and stretched out to sleep with the image of the three bodies dancing lasciviously through his mind.

Sometime during the night he woke. He was sitting up with the Colt in his hand and his eyes scanning the darkness for sign of danger before he realised what had broken his sleep. From farther down the stable there was a low murmur of conversation. It was too indistinct for him to catch the exact gist, but he heard his name mentioned twice. He wondered why the nuns should be talking about him in the middle of the night. And that wondering raised several unvoiced questions.

Like why three nuns would travel unaccompanied through dangerous country.

And why they had to go north of the border to find religious artifacts.

And why they had been so calm about the killing of

Ned Thatcher and Aaron Grange.

That last question gave him the most trouble. He hadn't thought much about it at the time : he was too used to killing to spend time dwelling on death, but the nuns – they said – were devoted to life. Yet not one had batted an eyelid at the deaths. It was, now he came to think about it, as if they had expected him to appear and kill the two men. There had been no panic, no screaming apart from that first warning cry. And there had been no talk of praying for the dead men, just the determination to move on as fast as possible.

Azul knew little of nuns or their way of life, but he was sure it did not include the casual acceptance of death.

He holstered the Colt and lifted to his feet. The straw crackled under his moccasins and for a moment the voices dropped. Then the grey horse shifted in its stall, disturbing the straw so that Azul's movement was lost and the nuns began to talk again. The halfbreed eased quietly out from the bay and slipped round the walls into the next stall. He was too cautious to come too close to the nuns, preferring to hunker down inside a pen a few up from theirs and hear whatever he could.

What he heard gave him more cause for concern, fragmentary though it was.

'What happens when we get home?' asked Sister Maria.

'We pay him.' That was Teresa.

'He'll see,' said Julia.

'Maybe not . . . but anyway . . . can he do?'

'Trouble . . . lead them to us . . . dangerous.'

'Leave it to me . . cross the border . . . forbidden.'

'Texas Rangers . . .'

'Listen to him? . . . trouble. Won't . . .'

'. . . like it. Kill . . .'

'. . . worry . . . sort it out . . . me.'

There was a murmur of assent and then the voices died away. Soon there was the soft sound of breathing as the three women settled back to sleep. Azul drifted back to his own stall and stretched on the soft cushion of straw with his eyes wide open and his mind working.

Whatever the nuns had been talking about didn't sound like three sisters taking religious artifacts back to their convent. Exactly what the purpose of their mission was, he couldn't tell. But he sensed there was something wrong with it. And that maybe the answer lay in the wagon.

He got back to his feet and sneaked silently out of the stable. The night was dark and cool. The sky was a big, wide spread of velvet blue-black pricked through with stars. Marisco was sleeping, and dawn was still a few hours away. The halfbreed went over to the wagon.

It was backed up against the corral fence, the tongue pointed south. Moisture was condensed on the tarpaulin, and the knotted ropes hung dark against the silvery grey of the canvas. Azul checked them. They were lashed down with professional skill, holding the load and the canvas firmly in place. He spent time working on the fastenings securing the tail-end of the canvas, careful to make no sound. It took him a while before he had enough of the heavy material cleared that he was able to check the stuff beneath. And when he did, he saw only a stack of ornaments and trunks. The ornaments were religious gilt-winged figures and effigies of Christ. When he touched them and tapped them, they rang solid in the still night air. When he opened a trunk, it contained religious books, layered – so far as he could tell without removing the whole tarpaulin – in stacks the depth of the trunk. Feeling none the wiser, he settled the canvas back in place and knotted the ropes in position again.

The only way to find out what the nuns were doing, he decided, was to stay with them.

He went back to the stable and fell asleep.

Dawn broke with the threat of rain darkening the eastern sky. They ate breakfast in the cantina and started out again as stormheads began to build on the horizon.

'How long now, mister Gunn?' asked Teresa.

'Three days to Santa Rosa,' answered the halfbreed. 'Unless the storm catches us. After that, I'm not sure.'

'Our convent is close to there,' smiled the nun, though a hint of worry showed on her face. 'We can find local men to take us on.'

'I'd thought to take you all the way,' said Azul. 'I thought that was our deal.'

'Santa Rosa will be fine,' answered Sister Teresa. 'Quite far enough.'

'I never seen inside a convent,' said Azul.

'Men are not allowed,' said the woman. 'I shall pay you off when we reach the town. Then you can make your way back.'

The last part of the sentence was said firmly, leaving the halfbreed in no doubt, but a great deal of curiosity. He said nothing, just shrugging and touching his hat.

They moved on into the start of the high country. The foothills gave way to real mountains, the flanks of the Jornados lifting seven and eight thousand feet above them, breaking into a series of jagged peaks that were already topped with snow. The lush greenery of the lowlands gave way to the harder timber of the uplands, deciduous timber covering the ridges where the trees were able to find rootage amongst the cuts in the solid stone. Great sweeps of bare rock hung over their path, the trail winding steadily upwards past falls of scree and thickets of timber, around landslides and fallen boulders. It was narrow, often little more than the wagon's breadth wide, and at times so steep that Azul fastened his rope on the tongue to drag the team upwards as the nuns pushed from behind. The nights were cold and the days warm with the sweat of sun's shine and effort. Nine times they chocked the wagon and manhandled it over broken stretches, where recent falls had carved channels through the trail. Eagles circled lazily above them, and from the timber covering the ridges foxes and bobcats cried in the night.

After two days of solid effort they reached a plateau.

It was a wide circle of grass and pine, ringed by the mountains. From the rimrock, it was possible to see their trail winding down in serpentine curves to the foothills. The start was lost in heat haze, parts of the upper trail obscured by low cloud. The air was thin and cool, the grass dry and crumbly underfoot, nourished by a narrow stream that ran down from the peaks to trickle clean and clear and blue across the centre of the meadow.

They halted there. And that was the time the Yaquis chose to attack.

The wagon was parked close to the stream. The nuns were sleeping underneath, blankets fastened to the wagon's sides to form an enveloping curtain. The horses were hitched to a tether line alongside the stream, and Azul was rolled in his own blanket close by the fire.

It was soon after dawn. The air was cool and there was a thin mist rising from the stream to spread grey moisture against the light of the rising sun.

The sound of hoofbeats woke the halfbreed: they drummed up through the ground into his ears, so that he rolled over with his hands clutching at the Winchester cradled beside him. Dew freckled his face, and he wiped it clear as he peered into the mist.

Some sixth sense turned him round as the first Yaqui came in on foot, clutching a machete that was lifted up for a killing stroke that would have cut Azul's head from his shoulders had he been still asleep. Instead the halfbreed's rifle barked as the blade rose. The .44 calibre bullet took the Yaqui in the chest, hurling him backwards as it smashed into his scapula and deflected off into the right lung. It lodged against the clavicle, spinning the machete out of the tanned hand as nervous shock jerked the muscles rigid. The Indian fell back with blood staining the front of his rawhide shirt and more coming from his mouth and nostrils.

Azul spun round, still on his knees, and fired twice more at the riders he saw coming through the mist. A horse screamed and went down, pitching the man astride its back forwards in a rolling fall that broke his neck and left his body crushed by the descending weight of the dying horse. A second Indian pitched backwards over the withers of his mount with his hands reaching up to clutch at the hole in his throat. And then Azul turned again as he heard the pad of feet loping towards him.

He shot the Yaqui in the groin, spilling the Indian's manhood out through the tail of his loincloth in a long streamer of pulped flesh and bright crimson blood that doubled the man over with both hands clutched tight against his crotch and a long, shrill yell echoing from his throat. The second was on him before he had a chance to lever a fresh shell into the Winchester.

Azul rolled as the machete came down, taking the force of the blow on the underside of the rifle. Shards of wood splintered from the underpinnings, and the halfbreed drove his feet out straight and fanning between the Yaqui's legs. The Indian was already off-balanced by his own blow, and Azul's counter movement lost him all his advantage. He came down in a heavy tumble onto the halfbreed's body. Azul pushed him clear and let go the Winchester. The Yaqui rolled back, reaching out to clutch Azul's right wrist. The halfbreed let him hold it, ignoring the holstered Colt as he snatched the Bowie knife clear of the sheath and drove it left-handed into the Indian's ribs.

The wide-bladed knife grated on bone as it went in. Azul twisted it, spreading ribs apart as the razor-sharp tip tore up internal organs. The Yaqui's hand slung the machete past his neck, sinking the heavy blade into the ground as the halfbreed withdrew the Bowie and slammed it up against the Indian's head. The point went in through the soft bone of the temple. It severed the nerves linking the eyes to the brain. The point emerged on the far side of the skull as the Yaqui's eyes popped out from the sockets, both orbs falling loose where the Bowie had cut through the tendrils of sinew and nerve. The Yaqui screamed and writhed clear of Azul's body, his hands lifting up to the bloody holes in his face. The movement dragged the blade harder into his skull so that it came loose on a huge welter of blood as the corner of his left eye was split entirely apart.

Azul left him screaming to turn and snatch the Winchester up from the ground. As he did it, the two glaucous orbs fell from his shirt. He ignored them, triggering shots at the horsemen still coming in through the mist.

There were two riders and two men still on foot. A lance cut air close beside the halfbreed's head, and he rolled over, triggering off a shot that lifted the horseman from his saddle with blood spreading over his back as he pitched forwards over his pony's neck and fell down full-length on the ground.

There was a moment of silence, and then a screaming man came out of the mist with a tomahawk lifted up to cleave Azul's skull. The halfbreed shot him in the chest, the force of the bullet hurling him back while Azul stood up and ran towards the wagon.

He reached the underside and found all three nuns levelling hideaway derringers at the attackers.

'Guard the horses,' said Sister Teresa. 'Please !'

Azul nodded and crawled out to the tether line. He began to drag the animals in, when a Yaqui came running up with a Colt's Dragoon spitting flame through the fog. Azul shot him, using the rifle one-handed; planting a .44 calibre slug through the Indian's belly so that his spine got shattered and he doubled over to somersault facedown at Azul's feet.

The last Yaqui chose to attack the wagon. He got in close before Azul shouted a warning and the three little handguns blasted in unison, sharding a gaping hole in the Indian's chest that spilled him backwards from the waist up as instinctive motion sent his feet pounding out from under him. The hatchet he was carrying spun loose from his hand, and then his feet outpaced his torso and he skidded to a halt with blood pumping from the front of his shirt and his heels drumming a death dance on the ground in front of the wagon.

Azul crouched down beside the horses, his rifle angled out into the mist.

There was silence again, and then the sun came up, transfusing the grey fog with bright red light that became gold as the mist dispersed. The bodies of the Yaquis were spread over the grass. Two of the Indians' horses lay dead. Azul led the wagon team and his own mount over to the solid bulk of the vehicle.

And Sister Teresa came out from underneath, followed by Julia and Maria. Her wimple was pulled back from her face, exposing the long, dark brown hair. Her eyes were wide and her arms open. She clutched the halfbreed, burying her face against his shoulder as she wrapped her arms around him and pressed herself against him.

'Thank you,' she moaned. 'God bless you. Thank you.'

Azul let go the horses and set his left arm around her shoulders.

Before he could say anything, she was laughing and crying at the same time.

'You saved us. We'd be dead, if not for you. Thank you.'

He didn't know what to say. Nor how to take her gratitude. So he just stood there and enjoyed the feeling of her body against his. And after a while she let go and stepped back. She looked embarrassed, adjusting her headgear so that her hair was hidden again under the fastenings of the wimple and she looked once more like a serene nun.

The other two followed her, their faces pale as they smiled their thanks at the halfbreed. He noticed that their fingers worked nimbly at the little derringers, breaking the pistols open and extracting the spent cartridges with a deftness that suggested an unexpected familiarity with the pistols. They fetched fresh loads from inside their robes and dropped the bullets into the twin chambers. Then the derringers were hidden again. Azul began to reload his own weapons.

'How come you carry guns?' he asked casually.

'For protection,' murmured Sister Teresa.

'I thought you said your faith was protection enough,' grunted Azul.

'Sometimes,' answered Sister Teresa evenly, 'it needs a little help.'

Azul shrugged, even more confused by the strange attitude of the three sisters. Then Teresa touched his arm and asked, 'Shall we get going? There may be more of them.'

'Don't you want to bury them?' asked the halfbreed. 'Maybe say a prayer over them?'

For a moment the nun looked confused. Then she nodded, calling the others to her. Azul began to settle the nervous horses into the traces as the three black-clad figures knelt and began to intone what might have been a prayer. It was voiced too low for Azul to make out properly, and when it was done they stood up and came

35

over to the wagon without a backward glance at the corpses.

'It will take too long to give them Christian burial,' announced Teresa. 'Anyway, they were heathens. Children of the Devil. Best we leave them and press on.'

Azul was reminded of something old Sees-Both-Ways, the Chiricahua shaman had once said to him. It was after a wandering priest had chanced on the *rancheria* and spent several days extolling the virtues of Christianity to the sceptical Apaches.

The whiteman's faith is a strange thing, Sees-Both-Ways had told the young man. *They preach of peace on Earth, yet kill those who oppose them. They say that the meek shall inherit the Earth, yet scorn the meek man for a coward. They say it is wrong to kill, then punish men with death. It is very hard to understand what they mean. I do not think they understand themselves.*

Azul looked back at the nuns as he led the way forwards across the meadow and agreed with the old man's words.

'For nuns,' he muttered to himself, 'you sure got strange habits.'

CHAPTER FOUR

The weather changed as they came closer to Santa Rosa, the warmth of the Indian Summer giving way to the shifting patterns of Autumn. The stormheads Azul had seen back in Marisco seemed to trail them over the empty high country, great black reminders of the impending Winter. And just before they reached the settlement, the storm broke.

It was a cool day, the air still and silent with that curious absence of sound that precedes a bad storm. The horses were fretful, sensing the threat of rain, and Azul kept the wagon to as fast a pace as was possible over the rough terrain. He halted at the foot of a steep gradient that climbed precipitously to the rim of a pine-topped ridge and stared dubiously at the path.

'What's wrong?' called Sister Teresa. 'Santa Rosa is the other side.'

'It'll take a day to climb that.' Azul pointed at the narrow trail. 'I don't want to get caught up there when the storm breaks.'

'Can't we make it before?' she sounded anxious.

'Don't look like it.' Azul turned to gesture at the big black clouds roiling across the sky. 'That's coming fast.'

As though to emphasise his words, a cold wind gusted over the flat, rustling the grass and setting the horses to stamping. A brief flash of sheet lightning illuminated the underside of the stormheads, followed seconds later by the grumble of thunder.

'We must.' Sister Julia stood up on the wagon seat. 'We're expected.'

Teresa ignored her as she turned to Azul. 'Are you sure? They'll be waiting for us.'

'They'll wait a long time if that storm hits us up there,' said the halfbreed. 'We'll halt down here.'

'No!' Julia's voice was urgent. 'Linda said . . .'

'Sister Julia!' Teresa's voice cut through the protest, stopping the fair-haired nun in mid-sentence. 'The Reverend Mother will understand. It is more important that we deliver the wagon safely. That's right, isn't it, Sister Maria?'

The dark nun nodded silently, her big eyes hooded, and Teresa turned to smile at Azul. 'It's agreed, then. We'll wait out the storm here.'

Azul dismounted and led the way over to the face of the bluff. He guided the wagon in close against the rock and unhitched the team, using his rope to fashion a tether line. He unsaddled the grey and slung his gear beneath the wagon, then he set to fashioning a kind of curtain from the groundsheets so that the underside of the wagon was sheltered.

'How long will it last?' asked Teresa.

Azul shrugged, looking up at the sky. By now it was unnaturally dark and the grumbling sound was getting louder as the wind got stronger. 'Hard to say,' he murmured. 'A few hours. A day, maybe.'

Sister Teresa started to say something, but changed her mind. The wind was whipping her robe tight against her body, outlining the contours of her breasts and hips. Azul was reminded of the feel of it against him; the way it had looked back at the river.

'Best get under the wagon,' he said. 'It looks bad.'

It was.

The wind began to buffet the canvas coverings, bulging them inwards, then straightening them with a series of popping, whiplash sounds that got abruptly lost under the tumultous deluge of rain. The wind howled, driving water in through the gaps so that the three nuns huddled together against the wheels closest to the rockface, farthest from the downpour. Sister Maria screamed as an enormous peel of thunder shook the wagon and brilliant white light sizzled in the air outside. Azul crawled to the front, peering out at the horses. Each animal was hobbled, as well as being fastened to the tether line, but they were still stamping around with rolling eyes and laid-back ears as they watched the lightning dance across the flat.

It came on flickering insect legs of light, like some gigantic sky-beast stalking the hills in search of prey. Multi-legged it was, like a centipede, with darting tongues probing in front. Its belly was pure black, shading to an ugly blue where the fire lit the edges, and from all the underside there came the pelting rain and the constant roar of angry thunder. A many-tongued fork struck the rimrock, and from above there was a second sound added to the fury of the storm : the sound of tumbling rocks. A whole chunk of cliff came down in pieces, shards large as a man's torso mixed in with the tumbling shale and two riven trees. Fragments bounced heavily off the tarpaulin covering the wagon, but the main part of the avalanche cascaded out over the grass.

Azul cursed as he saw the horses drag the tether line free of one fastening. He went out into the storm.

It was like struggling through a nightmare. The instant he stepped clear of the wagon he was drenched. The wind drove rain against his face so that he was partially blinded, raising one arm to protect his eyes. The lightning dazzled him, and the bellow of the thunder dinned inside his head so that he became deaf. He grabbed the loose end of the rope and staggered back towards the wagon, letting the gale carry him forwards. He got the line hooked around a wheel and began to pull the horses in. Panicked, they fought the drag of the rope, and the half-breed was hauled over, losing his footing on the slippery grass so that he landed heavily on his back. He climbed to his knees and braced both feet against the wheel, using all his strength to fight the frightened animals until he had sufficient purchase to knot the rope tight.

Soaked and shivering, he crawled back under the shelter of the wagon.

'Sweet Jesus!' said Sister Julia. 'I could use a . . .'

'Cup of coffee,' finished Teresa. 'But I don't think there's much chance.'

'None,' grunted Azul, wiping water from his long hair.

The storm went on. It went on for most of the day. Azul stretched on the ground, oblivious of the damp, and went to sleep with the stoicism of an Apache warrior while the three women sat huddled and shivering, scarcely able

39

to talk for the cannonades of thunder.

It was the absence of sound – or, rather, its lessening – that woke the halfbreed.

He sat up, aware that the roiling tumult outside had died away. Somewhere far off he even heard a bird singing. He rolled over and crawled from under the wagon.

There was a soft rain falling now, and over towards the edge of the hills a rainbow was spreading multi-coloured light in a great arc across the sky. The storm was gone away to the southeast, almost lost beyond the folds of the mountains. There was no wind, and as he went over to the horses, the rain ceased and more birds joined the first songster. The sun came out and the grass covering the flat began to steam. Azul fetched blankets from the wagon and began to rub down the horses.

'Can we leave now?'

Sister Teresa came out from under the wagon with Julia and Maria close behind her. Azul shook his head.

'No.' He went on scrubbing the animals. 'The trail needs to dry out. The horses are frightened.'

That didn't apply in the case of the grey stallion. Trained by Azul, it was ready to go anywhere an Apache mustang would attempt; but the wagon team was a different proposition.

He looked up at the sky. 'It's close on sunset: we'll spend the night here. Get dried out, then start come morning.'

Sister Teresa didn't look happy about the decision, but she didn't say anything. Just nodded and began to wring the water from her robe.

There was no chance of making a fire, so the nuns stayed wet. They also stayed silent, as though something was on their minds they didn't care to discuss in front of the halfbreed. He saw to the horses and then shifted the wagon so that the driest patch of ground got a chance to dry further in what was left of the sun. Azul went off into the timber flanking the ridge and stripped naked. He squeezed the water from his clothes and then beat them with a pine branch until they were as dry as he could hope to get them. Then he went back to the wagon and checked his weapons while the women prepared food.

He broke the Colt down and dried the parts that were moist. There weren't many because the gun was constructed well enough to take a soaking and still work. But he preferred to be safe, so he dried it all out and put oil on the moving parts and a fresh load into five chambers. Then he went over the Winchester, taking the same precautions with the shells.

By the time he was finished, the nuns had done eating, so he swallowed jerky and biscuits and settled down to sleep with a pale moon rising over the sky like a laughing face.

And in the morning they started up the ridge.

It was slippery. The storm had washed dirt and loose timber down, so the going was slow. In places there were gaps where lightning had torn junks of the rock away. And twice they halted to shift fallen trees from their path. Several times Azul needed to shove the wagon, with Julia and Maria helping him, as Teresa led the wagon team and the grey stallion up the slope.

They reached the rim as the sun was going down, bathing the pines in red light that looked warm but felt cold in the breeze blowing over the uplands.

Sister Julia wanted to push on, but Azul persuaded Teresa that it would be better to stay over. Get a fire going, so they could start down to Santa Rosa with full bellies and dry clothes.

He gathered timber as the nuns prepared food.

The fire was bright and high. Everyone was dry, the three women agreeing that it was better to sit in their chemises rather than stay damp, so that three habits hung like sombre laundry from Azul's rope as they ate canned beans and the two rabbits he had shot.

There was nothing enticing about their state of undress : the chemises were grey from the rain and covered the women as effectively as the darker robes, fastening high at the throat and covering their arms and legs about as far as was possible. Besides which, the derringers were in obvious position.

The only discrepancy – apart from the hideaway guns – was their hair.

'We are noviates,' explained Teresa, when he asked; casually. 'One of the reasons we were sent to fetch the relics was to prove our faith. Thanks to you, we have been able to do that.'

Azul didn't know enough about nuns to argue.

'Now we can enter the Sisterhood,' Teresa continued. 'And when we reach the convent, we shall say a Mass for you. For saving us.'

They reached Santa Rosa the next day.

Beyond the rimrock the mountains spread in a hogback that faded down into a sheltered valley. There was a wide trail leading down to a river that ran east to west along the bottomlands, the slopes covered with pine and small patches of terraced farmland. The facing slope was gentle, thick with plantations of corn and vegetables. On the crest there was a grim white building, its walls spreading along the natural folds of the terrain to form a fortress-look. A bell glinted distantly in the sunlight.

'Our convent,' said Sister Teresa. 'You can see how close it is to Santa Rosa.'

Azul looked down the valley.

Beneath the forbidding aspect of the convent there was a town. It was spread along the river, sun's light glancing off tiled roofs and adobe walls. It was surprisingly large for so lonely a stretch of country.

'The farmers ship their produce down the river,' explained Sister Teresa. 'Our convent helps them.'

'How?' asked Azul, bluntly.

'We are respected,' smiled the nun. 'People buy the goods of Santa Rosa.'

'Because of you?' asked the halfbreed.

'Because of us,' said the sister. 'Because of what we mean.'

The attitude of the peons Azul saw as they rode in bore out Teresa's statement. The men and women working the fields stopped as the wagon went by, waving and bowing as they saw the three nuns on the drive seat. They halted their labours and crossed themselves, and went on waving until the wagon was out of sight.

Inside the town it was much the same.

Santa Rosa was big. There was a wide street with a fountain at the centre, a statue depicting a nun holding a cornucopia that trickled water down over the marbled folds of the habit, set in the centre of a wide plaza. Facing the fountain there was a mayor's office with a fat man with waxed moustaches coming down the steps. The streets leading in boasted three cantinas that Azul had seen, and at least two bordellos. The central plaza had a bank and a stage office either side of the mayor's palace, then a spread of stores : hardware; dry goods; saddlery; a milliner's. On the facing side there was a hotel and a cantina; a stable; a second bank; and another cantina.

The man with the waxed moustaches came down the steps from the marbled facade decorating the front of his office. He was flanked by two men wearing wide sombreros and pearl-handled pistols. He was short and fat, his hair greased back in shiny strands over his skull. The men either side of him were tall and lean, with the hungry look of natural-born killers. Their hands stayed close to the butts of the Colts holstered on their hips.

'*Las hermanas*,' said the fat man. 'Welcome home. And with a friend.'

'Our guide,' answered Sister Teresa. 'He got us over the mountains.'

'*Madre* Linda will be pleased to hear that,' said the fat man. 'Does he speak Mexican?'

'*Seguro*,' said Azul. '*Hablo Mexicano de tal palo tal astillo.*'

The fat man blushed underneath his tan and began to twirl the ends of his moustaches. He changed to American.

'Put your wagon in the stable. Then we can talk.'

Sister Teresa nodded, and the halfbreed turned towards the livery.

'Forgive me, *señor* Gunn. I did not know that you speak our language.'

Luis Felipe de Aranjuez smiled at Azul and passed the bottle down the table.

'*De nada*,' murmured the halfbreed, smiling back at the fat little mayor. 'Why should you?'

'Mister Gunn saved our lives,' said Sister Teresa. 'Once when we were attacked by Americans, and then again when Yaquis tried to kill us. We would not have got here, but for mister Gunn.'

'Bravo,' said the mayor. '*Heróe*!'

Azul shrugged and glanced down the long table. Aranjuez was at the head, Sister Teresa to his right, and Azul on his left. Two bankers were set between them, then Sisters Julia and Maria, and then other civic dignitaries.

He picked up his glass, wondering why the hired hand was getting the regal treatment accorded the favoured nuns of Santa Rosa.

'What did you do?' asked the mayor. 'That business with the Yaquis worries me.'

'Killed them,' said Azul, wondering if he had had too much to drink. 'What else do you do when someone's trying to kill you?'

'Quite.' Aranjuez smiled at Sister Teresa. 'But I am worried about Indians in general. I had thought this area was safe from attack.'

He refilled Azul's glass as he said it. And the halfbreed picked up the wine as the mayor and the nun exchanged a glance.

'Mister Gunn was a saviour,' said Teresa. 'Had he not been with us, we would never have got here.'

'Then I owe you a debt,' said Aranjuez. And climbed to his feet : 'To *señor* Gunn!'

Everyone drank.

Azul stared at his glass. He was accustomed to drinking whisky or beer. Could handle the lethal *tiswin* the Apaches drank when they could get it. But wine was something else. That he wasn't used to; and that was what Aranjuez kept pressing on him. White wine with the thin soup of the first course of the celebratory meal, then more with the fish; then red with the savoury game, followed by more red with the meat. Then some kind of sweet, thick wine with the cheeses that were produced.

He tried to refuse the glasses, but Aranjuez and Sister Teresa urged him on. And it seemed to have no effect on them, so he followed suit. And before long he felt his head swimming and his eyes closing.

'I think our friend has had enough.'

The words came through a mist of faces and voices, and Azul was vaguely aware of his head lolling back against his chair. He looked up, forcing his eyes to open on Sister Teresa's face.

'Shall I get you to bed?'

The question surprised him. And pleased him at the same time.

'Sure,' he said; thinking about the body back at the river. 'Why not?'

He was aware of two men helping him to his feet, but mostly aware of Teresa's arm around his shoulder as he went up the stairs.

He got onto the landing and saw a door in front of him.

'All right,' he said, dismissing the men. 'I can get in from here. The Sister can handle me from now.'

There was a pause while he hung from the sides of the door. Beyond, he saw – just – a wide bed with white sheets and high-stacked soft pillows. He walked towards it.

The men left the room.

He heard the door close and turned to see Sister Teresa framed against the panelling.

'You'll be all right,' she said. 'Let me help you.'

He did. Enjoying the feeling of her hands removing his clothes. He lay back on the bed.

'Wait,' she said.

And he did. While a slow, heavy darkness closed down on his mind, like quicksand sucking him in as he thought about Teresa and nuns and their curious habits.

CHAPTER FIVE

Light replaced the darkness and there was a dull ache somewhere deep inside his skull. It became a real pain when he opened his eyes and saw sunlight filtering through the shutters covering the window. He sat up. Then groaned as the movement sparked fresh discomfort that made the room swim for a moment. His mouth was dry, the tongue furred and sour; he had difficulty focusing his vision. He closed his eyes again and pressed both hands against his pounding head, then, with an effort, he brought the room into focus. There was a washstand beside the bed, a tall jug standing inside a bowl. He grabbed it and drank off half the contents in a series of great gulps, then tipped the remainder over the back of his skull.

It was the third time he had been drunk.

Once, soon after he had passed his manhood tests to the satisfaction of the Chiricahua, his father had taken him to a saloon. *You can live like an Apache*, Kieron Gunn had explained, *an' you can handle most of the whiteman's ways. But this is something you gotta handle yourself. First hand.*

Why? Azul had asked. Not understanding.

There's folks think it's real funny to get an Indian drunk, Kieron had replied. *I want you to know what it feels like.*

He had bought a bottle of whisky and sat down with two glasses. The liquor had tasted sour, burning his mouth and filling his throat with a fierce heat that crept down into his belly and made his eyes water. The second shot had gone down easier, and when he swallowed the third the heat became pleasurably intense, like the warmth of a lodge fire on a cold Winter's night. He had been amused to find he was seeing two of everything, and after the fourth glass he was laughing. By the fifth his limbs had become disjointed, uncontrollable. Which seemed even funnier. And then, with a curious detachment, he had realised there was a ball of fire inside his belly that was climbing back up his throat as the room revolved about him.

He had gotten halfway to the door before he fell down on his knees and began to vomit.

The next memory he had of the event was the pounding in his head and the discomfort of his pony's spine jogging against his belly. He had thrown up again. And spent the rest of the day in a haze that alternated between the weird spinning sensation and sickness. It had not been until evening that he was able to hold down the coffee his father gave him, and even then he had not wanted to look at the food offered.

Now you know what it's like, Kieron had said. *Now you know how helpless it makes you. It's like riding a bronc: you don't get on until you know you can handle it.*

The second time had been in a small town north of the border, a place called San Jacinto, where a bounty killer had come looking for him.*

And this was the third – and last, he swore.

He hiked his wet hair clear of his face and squinted his eyes up against the light. The bed was ruckled, his clothes set out neatly on a chair. There was no sign of Sister Teresa, and he wondered if he had dreamt it.

But he knew he hadn't : the nun had been in the room. She had undressed him : a faint memory of her hands on his body fought its way up through the ugly feeling of the hangover. She had taken off his clothes and settled him on the bed. That much was a fact; the rest he couldn't be sure of : it might be drunk-dreaming – pure wishful thinking – or fact. It was impossible to tell. But either way, he enjoyed the memory.

He pulled on his clothes and set the throwing knife inside his moccasin. Buckled on his gunbelt, checking the Colt's load from pure habit. Then he went out of the room and down the stairs.

It was difficult going because each step rang inside his head, and his joints ached as he moved them, but he

See: BREED 13 – BOUNTY HUNTER!

reached the foot and stared around. The room was empty. The long table was still there, with a plate and knife and fork set on a linen napkin; a cup beside. There was a bowl of fruit at the centre. He sat down.

A servant appeared and asked him if he wanted breakfast.

'Coffee,' he said. 'Where is everyone?'

The servant shrugged and disappeared through a door. A few moments later Aranjuez entered the room.

'How do you feel?' asked the Mexican; solicitously. 'I do not think you are used to wine. Forgive me.'

Azul said, *'De nada,'* automatically. Then : 'Where are the sisters?'

'Gone,' said Aranjuez. 'Back to the convent. Sister Teresa left you this.'

He passed Azul a sealed envelope, bulked out by the contents.

The halfbreed broke the seal and fished ten ten-dollar bills out. They were new, the paper crinkly under his fingers. He dropped them on the table and began to read the note in which they had been wrapped. It was written in a smoothly-flowing script, the g's and y's and j's curlicued ornately.

It said : *My dear Mister Gunn, Thank you for everything you have done for us. Without you it would have been impossible to get home. Your money is here, but just as the Good Samaritan gained his reward later, so will yours come. Please forgive us for leaving without seeing you, but we, too, have duties. We wish you well, and will pray for you, just as we promised.*

It was signed with a flourishing *T*.

'You'll be going back,' said Aranjuez, 'I suppose?'

Azul shrugged, drinking coffee to still the ache the movement brought on.

'There's nothing for you here,' said the Mexican. 'This is a quiet town. Thanks to the convent.'

'Thanks to the convent?' asked the halfbreed.

The mayor smiled and stroked his moustache. 'Few people wish to make trouble under the shadow of the Sisters. They are a calming influence. There is nothing of interest for a man such as you. Besides, they paid for supplies to see you safely back across the border. It would be an insult to ignore that generosity.'

There was an implied threat in the words that registered only dimly through Azul's hangover. He drank more coffee.

'They have provisioned you well,' continued Aranjuez. 'Food; ammunition; even fodder for your horse. I have it outside now.'

'Thanks,' grunted Azul. 'That's real kind.'

'*De nada*,' smiled the mayor. 'I will send two men with you – in case there are still Yaquis about.'

'I'll be all right,' said the halfbreed. 'On my own.'

'No.' Aranjuez's voice was definite. 'I could not allow a man who has helped our town so much to chance it. My men will ride with you until it is safe.'

Azul shrugged, realising when he was beaten: 'All right.'

It was mid-morning when they set out. The two men Aranjuez had detailed off to escort the halfbreed were the two he had seen the night before. They both rode big stallions, and carried Winchester carbines across their hips. The muzzles stayed oddly angled towards Azul, and they rode slightly behind him; more like guards than guides.

They made better time than the wagon had been able to, getting up onto the hogback well before sunset and crossing the ridge to the start of the downwards trail as the sky got dark and the birds stopped singing.

'You can go back now,' said Azul. 'I'll be all right.'

'*El jefe* said to see you safe,' grunted the tallest *pistolero*. 'We shall take you another day.'

There was an ambiguity about the words that disturbed the halfbreed: set up all the earlier doubts he had felt churning around his mind.

'What's your name?' he asked.

'Juan,' said the *pistolero*. 'My friend is called Tonito.'

Tonito looked up from the fire he was building and grinned. 'We eat well tonight, *amigos*. *El jefe* gave us good beef. And this.'

He produced a bottle of red wine.

Azul shook his head, 'I'll take coffee. I drank enough of that last night.'

'*Hombre*,' said Tonito, still grinning. 'Don't you know that saying you got north of the river? What is it? A hair of the dog?'

'That's it,' agreed Azul. 'But right now I feel like the dog pissed in my mouth. And I don't want to taste it again.'

Tonito shrugged and drew the cork. He took a long swallow and passed the bottle to Juan. Juan drank deep and held the wine out to Azul. The halfbreed shook his head. Juan frowned, then handed the bottle back to Tonito.

'You don't like our wine?'

'Sure,' said Azul. 'I like it. I just drank too much of it yesterday.'

'Yesterday is all most of us got,' said Juan sombrely. 'You never know about tomorrow.'

'No,' said Azul. 'Not even about today.'

'I know we got good steak today,' said Tonito, doling out the meat. 'We eat well.'

They ate the steak and the two Mexicans finished off the bottle. Azul drank only coffee. Then Juan announced he would take the first watch; Tonito the second; Azul, the third.

The halfbreed stayed awake. It wasn't easy, the way he felt, but he did it anyway, mostly through sheer willpower. It was a discipline he had learnt from the Chiricahua, sitting out nights watching horse herds or enemy camps. He rolled himself in his blanket and kept his eyes open. They didn't necessarily focus on anything, so he got a kind of mental rest, but they stayed alert; as did his ears, assessing the sounds around the camp.

When Tonito came to wake him he felt lousy. His body was hot and itchy – much the same as his eyes – and he felt like taking a long bath in a cold stream followed by around ten hours honest sleep.

Instead, he sprang to his feet and went off to take his turn on guard. That way, he saw the sun come up : a huge red orb that lifted slow and stately from under the greyness of the dawn, pushing aside the curtains of vapour with a steady, irreversible progress that was, at first, slow, but then became faster as the light broke up the night. First, there was just a redness over to the east. Then the redness became the colour of blood, leavened with shards of pure brilliance that lanced up and out across the sky. Then the sun rose, huge and red and golden as multi-coloured rays spread in a fan-shape over the cloud. It got stronger. The red faded, giving way to the gold. Then the gold became pure silver, and the night got chased across the western horizon. Birds began to sing, and as the light got brighter they took flight. And as they did, the sky became blue, flecked over with soft white scuds of cloud.

Azul blew the fire into fresh life and set the coffee pot boiling again.

Then he woke the two Mexicans.

They exchanged glances as they realised they had been asleep; both of them.

'Coffee?' asked the halfbreed; wondering what the looks signified.

They went down the broken trail while the light was still dim over the flat. Dried out from the slickness of the storm, and cleared of rubble by Azul's efforts, it was easier and faster to negotiate than it had been coming up, with the wagon. They reached the place where Azul had killed the Yaquis late in the afternoon.

Parts of the bodies were still there. The bones had been broken, and ants were crawling over them to extract the nourishment of marrow and what little flesh had been left by the vultures and the coyotes. A flight of crows lifted into the air as they approached.

'It was here?' asked Juan.

'You see them,' said Azul.

'Yes,' said the *pistolero*.

And the action of his Winchester sprang loud in the still air.

Azul powered clear of the saddle as the heavy *click!* of the carbine echoed over the meadow. He went down on the right side of the grey horse, taking the reins with him so that the stallion screamed and fell down as the .44–40 calibre slug whined over its head.

He landed on his feet, right hand fisting the Colt's Frontier clear of the holster in a single flow of movement that dragged back the hammer and took up the trigger slack as he lined the muzzle on Juan's chest.

Trigger loosed hammer. Hammer fell on chamber. Fulminate erupted, igniting powder. And the powder exploded into the confines of the chamber, hurling raw power against the nub of the lead slug so that it was hurled down the grooved barrel of the gun, collecting velocity as it spun round and round until it reached the end and thrust out into the air on a clean, straight line that ceased at the centre of Juan's chest.

There the cleaness of the movement ended. The bullet hit bone. Splintered through on a deflected path, taking with it little pieces of the bone it had broken until it struck the softness of internal organs and the shards of bone imbedded as the slug went on, tearing up the softness until it struck another hard obstacle, which was Juan's spine. It was slightly flattened by then, but still had enough of a tip, and enough power, that it splintered two plates of bone and lodged against the retaining tissue beyond.

Juan screamed as nervous shock flung through his chest and jerked his muscles rigid. His arms flew high, letting go the Winchester as blood flowered over the front of his shirt. He went backwards from the saddle, his scream getting higher pitched as blood began to clog his vocal chords. Then pain struck his mind like a sledge hammer landing against his brain. The sky went dark.

Then red.

Then he felt fire climb up his back and knew that he was dying.

It was an unpleasant sensation, because he was not yet properly dead. It would have been better if he was, but he wasn't. Instead, he could feel the pain; taste the sticky, salty blood filling his mouth and his nostrils. He was still able to see. Could see the halfbreed Aranjuez had ordered him to kill lining the gun on Tonito. Could still feel the pain.

He screamed, drumming his feet against the ground as

the irrevocable darkness climbed up his back and began to join with the redness in his head.

When they came together, he spat crimson in a sticky spray against the sky and felt his eyes shutter tight as a greater darkness snapped down over his mind.

Tonito was slower. He had been waiting for Juan's cue, and only began to lever his carbine when the big man made the move.

It saved his life. In a way.

Azul shot Juan and spun round, angling the Colt on Tonito. He squeezed the trigger and saw his bullet ricochet off the guard of the carbine.

The force of the shot snatched the Winchester from Tonito's hands, lifting it clear as splinters struck his face and he felt the power of it topple him back and sideways in the saddle.

He started to reach for the pearl-handled Colt holstered for riding on his left hip. He even got his fingers around the butt. But by then, the halfbreed had come out from behind his fallen horse and crossed the distance between him and Tonito in a swift rush.

The Colt's Frontier swept up, barrel slamming hard against Tonito's knee. Then the muzzle blazed flame that scorched a line over the Mexican's wrist deep enough that his hand jumped, involuntary, free of the Peacemaker. At the same time, Tonito's horse was dragged over, lifted out of the rearing stance the gunfire prompted so that it fell heavily on its side, hurling the rider clear.

Tonito hit ground and saw stars burst before his eyes.

Then he felt his body lifted up and the ground hit his face again.

He reached down towards his holster. And a foot landed on his wrist, grinding it down against the dirt. And something sharp pricked the back of his neck.

'Your choice,' said Azul. 'Fast or slow.'

Tonito swallowed dirt and fear.

'I don't understand.'

The pricking on his neck turned into pain and he felt something warm and wet and fluid trickle into his shirt.

He recognised it as blood : his blood.

'Who told you to kill me?' demanded Azul. 'Why?'

'I don't know!'

It was a last chance : despairing and hopeless. Like turning a pair of deuces against a full house : no hope but to play it out.

The blade cut deeper. It stopped pricking and scored a line over his neck.

'I keep doing this,' said Azul, 'I'm going to cut your head off.'

Blood ran down Tonito's neck. He tasted it in his mouth. It was salty.

'Juan,' he said. 'Juan told me to do it.'

Azul picked him up by the hair and tossed him onto his back. Then the halfbreed straddled him, knees pinning Tonito's arms to the ground so that all the feeling numbed out of his hands and they felt like dead, aching appendages below the burning hurt of his upper arm. The hurt went on growing into his shoulders and he was only dimly aware of the halfbreed's feet pinning his legs to the ground.

'Juan was a *pistolero*,' said Azul. 'Like you. He took orders, not gave them.'

'He told me,' said Tonito, holding onto his useless bluff. 'I just did what he said.'

The knife came down slowly. It was very big, with a curved blade that angled to a point like a needle before it cut away into the recurve.

The hand that held it was very steady, even as it directed the blade against Tonito's face. It slid the blade slowly over Tonito's cheekbones, almost like a doctor cutting out a wart. There was no pain; not at first. Only a warmth on the Mexican's cheeks.

The pain came later, and Tonito screamed. He saw that he was blind. Rather, he didn't see anymore; only knew it because his eyes were loose of his face, no longer held inside the orbs of his skull by the flesh of his cheeks, but loosened by the slashing of his skin so that they wobbled on empty edges of bone.

'That can be cured,' said Azul. 'If I get you back in time.'

Tonito started to shake his head, but the pain was too much.

Made worse when the halfbreed said, 'There are ants. I might put them inside your eyes.'

'Aranjuez,' said Tonito, his voice slow and low as a funeral dirge. 'He told us to kill you. He said it would help the Sisters.'

'Why help the Sisters?' Azul asked.

'They help us,' moaned Tonito. 'They bring us money Santa Rosa was nothing before they came. They help us. We help them.'

'How?' as quietly as a sidewinder Azul inserted the question.

'Money' rasped Tonito. 'They bring money. Always. Like you.'

'Me?' demanded Azul. 'How did I bring them money?'

'I don't know.' Tonito pressed his hands against his eyes. 'They send nuns away and they come back with money. That's all I know. I've never been inside.'

'Inside where?' asked Azul.

'That godforsaken convent,' snarled Tonito. 'Christ Jesus! I wouldn't go in there now, except for my eyes. What you done to them.'

'Don't worry,' said Azul. 'There's a bright future.'

And he drove the Bowie knife deep between Tonito's ribs, slamming the point down into the heart so that the Mexican just sighed and died; quietly, almost as though he wished it.

CHAPTER SIX

Azul slept on the problem.

He left the bodies where they were and moved off into the trees. The dead Mexicans' horses watched him go, one moving to follow, but then changing its mind and returning to crop grass beside its companion. Eventually, Azul guessed, they would wander back to Santa Rosa, and Aranjuez would realise his men had been killed. It didn't matter much: Aranjuez would know something was wrong when Juan and Tonito failed to come back with news of the halfbreed's death.

He rode through the pines, following a narrow deer trail until he found a place where he could ascend the ridge. He climbed to the rim and made camp inside a thicket of new timber. The saplings grew in a circle around a patch of grass, dense enough to provide cover from the wind and watching eyes alike. Azul took the saddle off the grey stallion and hobbled the big horse. Then he spread his blanket on the ground and stretched out. The sleepless night and his hangover were combining to dull his mind, and before he decided on his next move he wanted to clear his thoughts. He closed his eyes and let sleep take him.

He woke when it was dark. For a few moments he listened to the night sounds, watched an owl drift slow and silent overhead, then went back to sleep. When he woke again, the sky was paling in the east. The air was chill, and a silvery blanket of dew covered the grass. He climbed to his feet, shivering in the cold, and set to making a fire.

Before long he was drinking coffee and chewing bacon, all the weariness gone as he thought about what Tonito had said.

There were parts that were obvious and parts that were

incomprehensible, like a jigsaw puzzle. He tried to fit them all together.

Aranjuez had ordered the two *pistoleros* to kill him because his death would help the nuns. Tonito had sounded frightened of the nuns. And he had said they brought money in to Santa Rosa. That Azul had helped them.

The only way he could have helped them was by bringing the wagon in. So: the wagon must have contained money.

But why should Aranjuez wish to kill him for that?

And where did the money come from?

Fragments began to slot together; pieces of conversation; attitudes. A vague picture began to form.

Novitiates, Teresa had said, sent out on some kind of mission. Each of them carrying a hideaway gun she knew how to use. Not one of them overly concerned with the sight of death, of killing. All of them anxious to get back to Santa Rosa.

And they had come from Ysabel, where Mexican bandits had raided the bank.

What was it Vickers had said about the bandits? They seemed to know where the money was, but never seemed to take it with them?

Azul reached a decision. He kicked the fire dead and saddled the grey horse. The sun was up all the way now, lighting the trees as he rode south towards Santa Rosa.

He cut back onto the trail until he struck the ridge north of the town. Going in alone would be hopeless, and he wasn't even sure the answers lay inside the settlement. He looked across the valley to the bleak configuration of the convent, then turned his gaze down the slopes, seeking a different trail that would take him around the town.

He found what he sought three miles along the ridge. A rock fall had broken the rim, spreading a fan of shale that was now grown over enough to provide safe footing down a steep slope that ended on a ledge. From the ledge to the river, there was a trail that looked like woodcutters had used it. It went down to the water, and on the far side there was another path leading up.

Azul walked the grey horse down the slope, then mounted where the ground got surer and rode to the bank of the river. The water was twenty feet wide here; maybe ten deep. It flowed fast, whitetops creaming the surface. He drove his heels against the horse's flanks and urged the reluctant animal out over the bank into the river.

The water was cold, the current striking from the east, drifting them downstream so that the stallion was forced to use all its strength to fight the drag as the halfbreed fought its head round to point on the flat section of the south bank where the other trail he had seen went up the far ridge. Halfway across Azul half-fell, was half-washed, from the saddle. He swallowed water and came up coughing with the reins in his hand. Instinct moved his legs and arms as he began to swim for the far bank, striking out ahead of the stallion, tugging the animal behind him.

He reached the bank and crawled on hands and knees onto the sun-dried mud. Then he braced both feet against the slush where the river washed the base of the mud flat and hauled the stallion in. The big horse came out of the water in a great spray of silvery droplets. It stared resentfully at the halfbreed, snorting irritably and shaking its head so that water cascaded in all directions. Azul gentled it down, then led it up the slope.

The mud gave way to firm ground ten feet farther on. There was a narrow path cutting round the edge of the ridge, hidden from sight of Santa Rosa by an outwards flinging spine of rock that came down like the blade of a knife from the hills. On the west side there was a trail going up. It was steep, not used by people anymore, but still firm enough that deer and goats might make the ascent. Azul followed it.

It was hard going. Riding was impossible, and for most of the climb he shifted crab-like up the slope, using hands and knees and elbows and toes to make the grade. He dragged the horse behind him, alternately urging it on and manhandling it upwards over the worst sections. Several times he simply put his shoulder against its rump and pushed it up.

It was close on sun's set before they reached the top.

There was a shallower slope stretching east and west, going out to join the knife-blade rim of the spine he had seen earlier. Timber was thick, pine needles crunching underfoot as he led the horse eastwards. Above them, the ridges of the Jornados lifted high and lonely, getting bare where the rock became too steep and too cold for trees to grow; shaded with snow along the uppermost combings.

To the east the ridge folded down into a series of shallow valleys, their sides softened by rainfall and the natural declivity of the land. Azul used the last of the fading light to get close to Santa Rosa and the convent above. He made camp in a small fold of ground that was shaded enough that his fire couldn't be seen from the town or the convent. He rubbed the horse down and then dried out his own clothes.

Then he went to sleep, not thinking about anything.

With the brightness of the morning sun shining over its walls the convent looked no more welcoming. It was built out along a wall of rock that folded steeply for fifty feet or more before striking the gentler terraces where the farmlands lay. There was a secondary ridge that lifted a hundred feet into the air, all of them smooth, slippery stone immediately behind, separated from the convent walls by a dry gully. The convent itself occupied a natural vantage point where the rock had faulted and jutted out a spar over the valley below. There was a trail winding up from Santa Rosa, narrow and steep, curling for a mile before it reached the frontage of the convent and bled out onto a small plateau. The plateau was maybe fifty feet across, ending on two sides in sheer drops, on the other, at the walls of the fortress-like building.

The convent had walls thirty feet high. Squared-off on the corners with built-up towers roofed over with wood. There was a big gate at the front: two solid-looking sections of metal-studded planking with a drop-bar behind and metal bolts for support. Beyond the walls there was an open space of intermingled sand and flower beds. A well. Then buildings. The buildings were clustered at the centre, timber and adobe structures that rested lower than the walls, never higher than two storeys, and mostly windowless.

Inside the frontal area Azul saw the wagon he had brought up from Ysabel.

The canvas was off it now, and the load was getting transferred to a storehouse.

Men were carrying the carved figures and the trunks of books. And the men wore guns: they looked like *pistoleros*.

More pieces of the jigsaw doubts came together. And the halfbreed decided to take a closer look.

CHAPTER SEVEN

The walls shone stark in the moonlight, sheer and bleak and forbidding. Along the upper levels the stone was crenellated to afford defenders a series of vantage points, but no guards were visible. It was as though the place felt itself secure from attack, safe on its commanding height and guarded by the town below.

Azul slipped his rope from his shoulder and began to swing the loop about his head. His first throw dropped the noose smoothly over a buttress and he hauled it tight. Then, bracing his moccasined feet against the stone, he began to clamber upwards. He got to the top and slipped through onto the catwalk spanning the inner sides of the walls. From here the convent looked even more like a fort, except for the absence of guards. There were stables built under the catwalk, tight against the walls, and the buildings at the centre had a cold, forbidding look, the windows shuttered with heavy wooden planks and the doors reinforced with metal. The place was mostly silent, only one building still showing light. Voices rang from inside, muffled by the shutters; too indistinct for him to make out what was being said. He went down a ladder to the ground.

The storehouse was across the open space, set slightly apart from the main bulk of structures. The halfbreed crossed the distance in a cat-footed run that fetched him up against the doors. They were wide and tall, built to accept a loaded wagon. And not locked. He eased one open and slipped inside.

Light filtered in through a series of small windows set high in the walls. It shone pale on a double line of stacked crates, a jumble of religious carvings that were piled haphazardly at the far end. Several looked to be broken, angels' wings torn loose from the bodies, limbs scattered like the debris of some heavenly battlefield.

He walked to the pile. And saw something shining bright gold in the cold wash of moon's light. It was a half-size figure of a winged man, the hands clutching a carved book, the face bent to study the blank pages. One wing had been removed, and where it was separated from the body gold glistened. Azul stooped to peer at the break : it was as though the angel was boned with gold. The stub extending from the shoulder was hollow, the interior filled with coins. New coins, fresh minted.

The wing lay at the figurine's feet. The wood was dark and hard. Where it was broken off, more coins glinted. Azul turned away, going over to the stacked crates. Drawing the Bowie knife, he prised one open. It was filled with books. He lifted one out. The title was *Lives of the Saints.* He opened it and stared in surprise at the pages. Between each printed page there was a note : one dollar, fives, some tens. The book must have carried around two hundred dollars between the covers. He picked up a second, and found the same alternation of text and money.

'Reading pays,' he murmured as he realised why the three nuns had been so anxious to get the wagon to the convent. And why the raiders always travelled light.

It was obvious now : a plan superb in its cunning, successful enough to deceive the Law and the Army alike. Who ever suspected a nun? They were invisible to suspicious eyes; inviolate. They could travel the Border towns without anyone realising they were watching the banks or the stagelines. Could pass information on with no questions asked. And then collect the loot and ship it back with the accepted anonymity of honest-to-God religious people. No questions; no suspicions : just nuns going about their business.

He grinned, admiring the daring simplicity of the plan.

And the door of the storehouse opened and three men came in with handguns pointed at him.

One was tall and very thin, dressed entirely in black. Like a dandified undertaker. He had long, dark hair, and a luxuriant moustache. His right hand held a long-barrelled Colt with a pearl-chased butt. The metal was silvered, polished to a high sheen. The hammer was all the way back, and one slender finger was tight on the trigger. The others wore conchos on their flared pants, and silver decoration on their short-waisted jackets. One was huge – a massive, bear-like man – with greasy ringlets hanging from under his sombrero and a thick beard covering his face. He held a Remington Army model revolver, the trigger guard cut away to accommodate his fleshy finger. The third was short and fat and held a S & W Russian in his left hand.

'*Buenas noches,*' said the black-clad man. 'Walk very slowly towards me. Try anything and I'll kill you.'

Azul walked slowly towards him.

'We found him in the store. It was a good thing Aranjuez warned us his men had been killed.'

The Mexican glanced at Azul, a thin smile decorating his saturnine face with a glint of malicious amusement.

The halfbreed was stretched over a table. His arms and legs were dragged down and lashed to the legs. His belly hurt where the bearded man had punched him, and his neck was starting to ache from the strain of holding up his head. He was inside the lit room, which seemed to be some kind of meeting hall. There were ten to fifteen *pistoleros* clustered around the walls, and as many women. He recognised Teresa and Julia and Maria amongst them, only now the sombre habits were gone, replaced by low-cut gowns with the dull, rich sheen of silk. He noticed that Teresa had piled her hair up, fastening it with a silver comb. Long earrings glittered against her slender neck.

But mostly his attention was taken up by the woman the Mexican addressed.

She was huge. Large as the bearded man, with bloated arms thrusting from the ruffled sleeves of a green dress that looked dangerously close to bursting at the seams. Her hair was red with henna, thrust up into a stack of incongruous curls above a pudgy, pig-like face. The skin was very pale, contrasting with the garish make-up that transformed her little eyes into dark pits, her mouth to a brilliant rosebud that puckered from the fleshy folds of her cheeks and chin like a third eye.

Her voice was shrill, the sibilant whistle of a child.

'Kill him,' she said.

'No!' Azul recognised Teresa's voice. 'Wait!'

The Mexican let the pearl-handled Colt drop slowly back inside the holster. The fat woman turned.

'What?'

'You can't,' said Teresa. Then, less surely, 'Please.'

'Why not?' asked the fat woman. 'He knows where we are. He knows how we do it. How long before he brings Texas Rangers to us?'

'He won't,' said Teresa.

'Damn' right he won't,' said the fat woman. 'He won't be able to.'

'Linda, please.' Teresa came across the room. 'Don't kill him.'

'Why not?' repeated the fat woman. 'He's dangerous.'

'He saved us.' Teresa came to stand beside the enormous red-head, one hand touching the other woman's arm. 'We'd never have made it back if it weren't for him. He saved us when those two men were going to rape us, then again when the Yaquis attacked.'

Linda looked away from Azul to Teresa's hand. The younger woman was moving her fingers gently, stroking the bloated, mottled flesh. Linda's eyes moved upwards, over Teresa's body until they fastened on the face.

'There's that,' she acknowledged.

'I'll make you grateful,' Teresa murmured. 'If you let him go.'

Linda moved her arm. For so large a woman she was very fast. Her right hand settled on Teresa's shoulder, the fingers digging deep into the flesh. Her left circled the younger woman's waist.

'You better,' she said in a soft whistle. 'If I do.'

Teresa leant forwards so that she was resting against the fat woman's body, her mouth close to Linda's.

'I will,' she whispered. 'I promise.'

Linda pushed her away. 'What's he mean to you?'

There was suspicion in her voice that Teresa dismissed with a shrug. 'Nothing. He saved our lives, that's all.'

Linda turned to stare at Julia and Maria. 'That right?'

They both nodded, and Maria said, 'We'd be dead if it wasn't for him.'

'Besides,' Teresa moved close against the fat woman again, 'he killed a man in Ysabel, and he's got a record in Texas. They don't like him: I don't think they'd listen to him.'

The fat woman's eyes travelled over Teresa's body again, then she shrugged. It was like watching maggots wriggle inside a sack.

'All right,' she said. 'I'll let him go.'

She came over to stand directly above Azul so that he could smell her perfume and the slightly sour odour of her breath. Her breasts bulged from the frontage of her dress like mammoth dumplings. 'You ever come back, I'll have you killed. You understand that?'

'Sure,' grated the halfbreed.

'Slow,' said the obese woman. 'So it hurts.'

Azul said nothing, just looking up into the porcine eyes glistening over the wobbling mounds of cleavage.

'Take him out,' said the fat woman, speaking to the Mexicans. 'Make sure he understands.'

'Si.' The thin man nodded. 'Es claro, Linda.'

They cut Azul loose from the table and hauled him to his feet. He caught one quick look from Teresa, rapidly averted as she turned to smile at Linda, and then he was dragged backwards out of the room.

They took him across the courtyard to the stables.

'You were lucky,' said the thin Mexican. 'Teresa saved your life. Linda would have killed you.'

'There's some fates worse than death,' grunted Azul, thinking about the way the fat woman had looked at Teresa and the implicit promise the younger woman had made. 'Putting a finger in a dyke can start the flood.'

The Mexican chuckled. And punched Azul hard in the belly.

The blow doubled the halfbreed over, filling his gut with pain so that he felt only dimly the smash of the giant Mexican's arm against his back. He went down on his knees, lifting his arms to protect his face as the others clustered round and began to kick him. He felt pain explode through his side, then choked on vomit as the boots thudded against his back. In a while the red, roaring pain coalesced into blackness and he slumped to the ground, unconscious.

When he woke it was morning. He winced, rolling over on a bed of straw that was redolent of vomit and manure. He opened his eyes, seeing the thin Mexican smiling at him.

'We'll let you go now,' said the man. 'But first there are some things you must understand.'

Azul sat up, staring at the bandit without saying anything.

'I am called Jose Cabra,' said the man. 'Santa Rosa is my town. This place,' he waved an arm to indicate the convent, 'is Linda's. We are both very bad people to cross. This time, you were lucky. Very lucky. Next time, you will die, so you better be sure there is not a next time. You understand?'

Azul nodded.

'All right,' said Cabra. 'Now I'll let you go. Just like Linda said.'

He stepped back, motioning two of his men to haul Azul to his feet. They grabbed his arms and yanked him painfully upright. Then they dragged him forwards into the courtyard.

'Just to remind you,' said Cabra, 'I'm giving you a present. It's something suitable to take from a convent.'

The bandits began to chuckle. The big bearded man came forwards holding two six foot lengths of timber that he stowed either side of a pack horse. Then they pushed Azul astride the pony and rode out through the gates of the convent.

They went down the trail and cut southwards, away from Santa Rosa to where a small stream sliced through the hills east of the main ridge. The country was wild, overgrown with trees and exotic plants. They rode for half the morning before Cabra called a halt.

'All right,' he said. 'This will do.'

They took Azul down from the horse and lashed his wrists to the poles. Then they lifted the lengths of wood upright and crossed them behind the halfbreed's back. The bearded man fastened rope around the centrepoint so that the two lengths formed an X shape. They tied Azul's ankles to the downwards end. The result was that the halfbreed was carrying a cross, balancing precariously with his arms dragged up painfully high above his head.

Cabra laughed and shoved Azul in the chest. Azul fell backwards, groaning as he hit the ground and lay spread-eagled. Cabra tossed his gunbelt down beside him.

'I let you go,' he chuckled. 'Just like Teresa wanted: we didn't kill you. You even got water here. *Adios.*'

The Mexicans mounted and rode away, laughing and pointing back at the spreadeagled figure of the half-breed.

Azul lay still until they were out of sight. The crossed poles dug awkwardly against his spine and he could feel his muscles knotting from the rigid posture of his stretched limbs. When they were gone he began to wriggle, desperately seeking some weakness in the crucifix. There was none: his own body held the thing in shape so that he was stretched taut, helpless as an overturned turtle.

The sun climbed across the sky. High above him, black dots against the azure, he saw the shapes of circling buzzards. Ants moved in busy columns over the sand of the stream's bank, investigating his body, traversing his chest, moving onto his face. The day was hot and still, the brilliance watering his eyes, drying out his mouth. A few feet away he could hear the stream gurgling over rocks.

He forced himself to remain calm, trying to think of some way of escaping the confines of the crucifix. Nothing came to mind, and he shut his eyes against the glare, making his body relax as best he could.

After a while, as the sun got hotter, he felt the cords binding his wrists grow tighter. At first it was an imperceptible pressure, but as the sun grew stronger it became distinct, cutting against his wrists so that his fingers grew numb and a dull ache began to form in the centre of his palms.

He turned his head, shaking ants loose from his face,

and squinted up and over at the topmost fastenings.

They were rawhide. He hadn't seen that before — not until the sun dried the cords and tautened them.

Rawhide shrunk as it dried. Wet, it expanded.

He listened to the stream.

Then be began to writhe, ignoring the agony that ground through his limbs as he jerked himself sideways. His feet were free enough that he was able to gain some small purchase on the side and that, combined with the humping movement of his body, enabled him to twist the cross slowly sideways.

It took a long time. It seemed longer: his movement was slow, crab-like; a spurt of slight movement followed by pain as he sucked in great deep lungfuls of air and tried to ignore the agony in his arms and legs and back. Then another spurt. More pain, until his whole body burned with it and only his anger kept him going.

Finally he was turned around. His head rested on the edge of the stream bank, his extended arms thrust out over the water.

The next part was the most dangerous.

He drove his feet against the sand, pushing out until he felt his body pivot on the edge of the bank and slide downwards. Cool wetness struck his hands, emphasising the burning ache of the sun-constricted rawhide. He felt the water touch his hair. Then the gurgling of the stream got louder as he slid down and his face went under.

He gasped, sucking air into his lungs as he made one final effort that shifted him all the way down the bank into the stream.

The water was cold, the current just strong enough to spin him round before the poles grated on stones and he was brought to a stop, resting full-length in the liquid.

He raised his head, ignoring the pain in his neck and shoulders as he fought for breath. The stream splashed over his face, watering his eyes and soaking his clothes. Soaking, too, the rawhide binding him to the crucifix.

And gradually he felt the bonds begin to loosen.

He was unsure how long it took for time had become unimportant. His entire being was concentrated on the effort of shifting his arms against the thongs, feeling the numbness of the binding replaced by the numbness of the cold.

And then his left hand came free. He wasn't aware at first. Not until the current shifted his arm down and round and he felt fresh waves of pain flood through his biceps and forearm. He lifted his head and stared at the arm. It didn't feel like it belonged to him anymore, and it was almost surprising to see it lift and move to the right.

Slowly, wincing at the stiffness of stretched muscles, he twisted his body until the fingers of his left hand touched the rawhide binding his right wrist to the pole. His hand was hooked claw-like, scrabbling awkwardly at the thongs. The stretching rawhide loosened further under the pressure of his grip and before long he was able to slide his right hand free. He sat up, groaning as he straightened, and reached down to where the hilt of the throwing knife still protruded from his moccasin. His fingers were numb, stiff as they clasped the hilt, and he needed both hands to hold the blade steady as he cut through the bindings on his ankles.

He crawled on hands and knees from the water, scrabbling up the bank to where Cabra had dropped his gunbelt. He touched the familiar butt of the Colt, an unspoken promise forming in his mind. And then he just lay there, still.

It was dusk by now. The sun was bathing the upper flank of the ridge in a wash of red light and the air was growing chill. The cold roused him from his torpor; that and his hate. He pushed up onto his knees, then staggered to his feet. He was shivering and his body ached from the beating and the crucifixion: he needed warmth and rest; food, too. He limped into the trees like a hurt animal seeking someplace safe.

He found the place close against the wall of rock. There was a split that angled a jumble of fallen stone in a semi-circle from the main line of the ridge. It afforded shelter and a screen of trees; more important, it afforded dry wood and several clumps of bushes bearing edible berries. He gathered wood and got a fire started. Then he plucked handfuls of the berries and huddled by the fire stuffing the sweetish fruit into his mouth. A pale, half-waned moon came up. He watched it, resting naked beside the flames as his clothes steamed on a framework of twigs. When they were dried out enough that the stream's chill no longer clung to them, he pulled them on and banked the fire high. Then he curled close to the heat and went to sleep, the Colt cupped in his right hand.

He woke to the misty coolness of the false dawn. Dew beaded the ground and from the stream there rose ethereal twists of vapour. He rebuilt the fire and went back to sleep.

The next time he woke, the sun was up. The sky was blue and clear and warm. He climbed to his feet, checking his body for signs of permanent damage. His wrists were scored where the rawhide had cut into the skin and there was still a dull ache in his ribs and stomach from the kicking, but so far as he could tell there was nothing broken or seriously injured. He crouched for a spell by the dying fire, enjoying the comfort of the warmth, then kicked it dead and began to walk northwards.

He followed the trail Cabra had taken until he estimated he was close to the southernmost limit of the plateau holding the convent. The slope to the west was steep and tree-covered : he began to climb.

Apache-bred, he was accustomed to moving on foot over mountainous terrain, but the effects of the beating and the crucifixion slowed him enough that he did not reach the rim until late afternoon. A curve of the hills went out before him, pointing north; westwards, the scarp grew higher and steeper. He followed the northern-pointing ridge on until he was above the convent. Timber grew all the way up to the edge of the down-slope and he moved through it to a position where he could study the place.

The slope, he noticed, was steep and bare, falling down into the gulley he had seen before that was flanked by the walls. There were people moving about inside the place : he recognised Cabra's black-clad figure, and that of Teresa. The wagon was parked under the overhang of a porch, and there were *pistoleros* lounging in the shade, drinking.

He stayed crouched on the rimrock for a while, thinking about his next move.

Then he moved back through the trees and began to work his way to where he had left the grey horse tethered.

The stallion greeted him with a fretful snicker that he muffled with his hands. Against the animal's protests, he mounted up and rode back along the line of the river until he was a safe distance from the convent. Then he made camp and fed the horse from the supplies left by Teresa.

In the morning he started north, skirting round Santa Rosa to pick up the trail leading back to Marisco and El Rio and Ysabel. He had decided how he would pay back Jose Cabra and the nuns.

'Sure,' he murmured to the big horse as it ate the miles in a fast gallop, 'I'll show them they crossed the wrong man.'

CHAPTER EIGHT

'You expect me to believe that?'

Major Ben Vickers combed fingers through his beard and frowned at Azul.

'You tell me you ain't interested in scouting for me. You kill a man. Three nuns save your life and hire you to take them south to their convent. Then you come back saying they're working with the Mex raiders. That don't sound right to me.'

'It's true,' said Azul. 'I saw what they got inside the convent.'

Vickers shrugged. 'All I got on that is your word.'

'Not all.'

Azul reached inside his vest, fetching out three coins. They glittered bright on the major's desk. New coins. Shiny with the fresh minting. Vickers scooped them up, his frown getting deeper.

'I got them from the convent,' said Azul. 'They were hidden inside a statue. There were books with paper money between the sheets.'

'Christ!' rumbled Vickers. 'Maybe you ain't lying.' He turned to Marshal Howe. 'Get Callender here.'

'He'll be at dinner,' said Howe. 'He don't like to be disturbed.'

'Show him one of these.' Vickers tossed a coin to the peace officer. 'And tell him I said to come fast.'

Howe looked at the coin, then looked at Azul. 'All right. If you think it's worth bothering him.'

'I do,' said Vickers. 'Now move!'

Howe moved and the major turned back to the half-breed.

'There just might be something in what you say.'

'There is,' said Azul. 'Who's Callender?'

'The banker,' grunted Vickers. 'Little feller with a big bark. He's been raising hell about the raids.'

'Now you got the chance to stop them,' said the half-breed. 'If you're ready to cross the Border.'

'I'm ready,' snapped Vickers. 'What I need is a better reason than your word.'

Azul shrugged and waited for the banker to appear.

Nathaniel Edson Callender was a short, fat, frog-like man. He had large ears that stuck out from the sides of his skull like flaps. His hair was thin, pasted in strands over a balding scalp that was mottled the same way as his hands. He wore gold-rimmed glasses on a long cord and a dove-grey suit. He was angry.

'This is one of the coins stolen from the bank,' he shouted. 'Why are you wasting time?'

'You sure?' asked Vickers.

'Of course I'm sure,' snarled Callender. 'There were three issues of new coin this year. El Paso and San Jacinto got some, we got the rest. This coin couldn't have come from anywhere but those banks.'

'It coulda come legal,' opined Howe. 'Couldn't it?'

'No!' Callender shook his head so hard the folds of flab on his jowls wobbled. 'I've been in contact with the other banks, and not one of us had time to issue the new minting before those bandits took it all. The only way these coins could show up anywhere is if they'd been stolen.'

Vickers and Howe exchanged glances. Callender caught the look and turned to face the Army officer.

'Where's this come from?'

'Same place as these,' said Vickers, showing the other coins.

Callender's face got purple. 'Where's the rest? Are you playing games with me, Major?'

'No,' said Vickers slowly. 'I don't think so. This man brought them in.'

Callender looked at Azul for the first time. 'A half-breed! Is he one of the gang? Have you arrested him?'

'He brought them in,' Vickers repeated. 'He says he knows who's been planning the raids and where the money is.'

'Then go after them,' barked the banker. 'Now! My

God! the bank is offering a reward of two thousand dollars. Besides, it's your duty. Do it!'

'Hold on,' said Vickers. 'I want to check some things first. To make sure the story's right.'

'What?' Callender demanded, his face suffusing into the colour of cooked beetroot. 'What?'

'You know of any nuns coming to the bank?' Vickers lit a cigar and began to suck smoke. 'Around the time of the raid?'

The banker scratched his head. Winced as his nails struck bare flesh. Then nodded, 'Yes. There was a Sister asked about money to buy land here for a convent. I told her we wouldn't have any money to invest until the new shipments came in. My God!'

He broke off, the purple of his face receding into a wash of white.

'You told her when?' asked Vickers.

'Yes.' Callender nodded. 'After all, a nun has to be honest. Doesn't she?'

'You tell her how much?' asked Vickers.

The banker shrugged. 'Maybe. She talked about money a lot, so I think I might have told her how much of a loan she could expect.'

He began to look embarrassed as Vickers stared at him.

'That wouldn't tell her about the new minting. Would it?'

'Work it out.' Vickers exhaled smoke in a thick, pungent cloud. 'You talked money with her. That coulda been enough to give her an idea of how much you was expecting. And when.'

'I guess so.' Callender swallowed hard. 'You think that's how the bandits knew?'

'It's the best bet we got,' grunted Vickers. 'Right now, it's the only one.'

'My God!' Callender's fat face trembled, all the anger gone now. 'This could ruin me. You've got to find them, Major! Find them and bring the money back.'

'I'll do my best,' said the officer. 'Thanks, mister Callender.'

'What are you going to do?' Callender asked nervously. 'When?'

'Leave it to me,' said Vickers. 'You just keep your mouth shut: I don't want anyone hearing about this.'

'God!' moaned the banker. 'Nor do I!'

'All right.' Vickers gestured at the door. 'You get on home. I'll let you know when something's happened.'

Callender stumbled through the door, all his bluster gone. Vickers turned to Azul.

'Looks like you could be telling the truth.'

Azul shrugged. 'You got one sure way to find out.'

'What you think?' this was addressed to Howe.

The peace officer shrugged. 'Don't see why he'd come back here unless he was tellin' the truth. What's he got to gain?'

'Yeah.' Vickers dropped his cigar into the spittoon. 'But let's talk it through.'

'Santa Rosa is here.' Azul inscribed an X on the map Vickers had spread out over the desk. 'Cabra said it was his town. The mayor is a man called Aranjuez. He sent two men to ride me clear and kill me. The convent is on this ridge.' He set a second X against the contour lines. 'It seems like it's run by a fat woman called Linda. It's built like a fort: be hard to get into.'

'You did,' said Vickers.

'I was one man,' answered the halfbreed. 'You take a whole bunch over the river and word'll go out. They'll be waiting for you.'

'All right.' Vickers shrugged. 'I'll take enough men to handle them.'

'You ain't allowed to cross the Border,' Howe reminded.

'Fuck the Border,' snarled Vickers. 'I'll cross it.'

'No.' Azul shook his head. 'It won't work that way. The only way you'll get men inside the convent is up the trail from the town. The way things are there, that means you have to take Santa Rosa first. You'd need artillery.'

Vickers shook his head and lit a fresh cigar. 'That I can't do. I don't have it, and I couldn't chance taking it over.'

'Breed got inside,' said Howe, not liking what he was

forced to admit. 'Maybe he knows a way.'

'Do you?' Vickers' question was direct. 'You got any ideas?'

'Maybe.' Azul pointed at the map. 'You dress your men in civilian clothes and send them over the river in groups. Separately. They meet up on the hogback.' He sketched a line down from the X marking Santa Rosa. 'Then you split them. One force goes into the town, the other works round to the high ground above the convent. When Santa Rosa's taken, both groups move in.'

'It could work,' Vickers acknowledged. 'How'd you learn to think like that?'

'With the Chiricahua,' said Azul. 'Fighting the Army.'

Vickers grunted and Howe suppressed a snigger.

'What do I do?' he asked.

'Stay here,' snapped the Army man. 'Keep things quiet so no-one goes asking questions about where I am. This fails, I lose my goddam commission : I get a court martial.'

'And if it works?' wondered Azul.

'I'm a goddam hero,' said Vickers. 'I could end up president of a bank.'

'Callender said something about money.' Azul grinned at the major. 'Who gets that?'

'We split it.' Vickers shrugged. 'That's fair.'

'How?' asked the halfbreed.

'He gets five hundred for keeping his mouth closed,' said Vickers. 'We get seven-fifty apiece. Plus, I'll put you on Scout's Pay for as long as it takes. Thirty dollars a month and all found.'

Azul nodded. He wasn't really interested in the money : what was important was taking his revenge on Jose Cabra and the nuns.

'All right,' said Vickers. 'It's gonna take a couple of days to get everything ready. I need to get my men kitted out, so you'd best stay quiet. Folks still don't like you round here.'

Azul nodded, 'It's a cross I have to bear.'

CHAPTER NINE

Azul spent the next two nights sleeping out on the prairie south of Ysabel.

Soon after dawn on the second day Vickers arrived with thirty men. The major was wearing broadcloth pants and a dirty shirt that was partially covered by a corduroy vest. A brown stetson covered his greying hair, and the only concession to Army regulations was the gunbelt he wore, flapped and holstered butt-forwards on his right hip. He carried a Winchester carbine alongside his saddle.

His men looked the same, except that they all wore Springfield singleshots on their saddles.

'All right,' said Vickers. 'Let's go. And for Chrissakes! do it right.'

They took off into the dawn mist, breaking up into separate groups as they approached the Rio Grande.

Vickers stayed with Azul. There were three men behind them: a sergeant with a thick Irish brogue called Kintyre; a trooper from the South called Enrow; and a Missourian called Yarbro.

Azul had agreed that one bunch should go over the river through El Rio, in case there was something to be learnt at the Border crossing.

'You?' said *El Patrón*. 'I didn't think you'd come back.

'What's he mean?' asked Vickers. 'What happened here?'

'Billy Angstrom's friends tried to jump the nuns,' said Azul. 'I killed them.'

'Christ!' said Vickers. 'You kill people everywhere you go?'

'Only when it's needful,' said the halfbreed, and arranged for them to get a meal and a place to sleep.

The following day they set off into the uplands

through the pale and misty wash of the dawn fog. This late in the year it was cold in the mornings, the sun not breaking through the cloud until relatively late in the day; and even then carrying with it the cold hint of Winter.

They climbed up towards Marisco, following the trail Azul had taken with the nuns, but skirting round the town to avoid warning the inhabitants of their passage. They mostly slept rough, out in the open, with Azul shooting game to provide fresh meat as a companion to the hardtack and salt bacon of Army rations.

And after a week they got to the hogback overlooking Santa Rosa.

'Christ!' Vickers grunted. 'I see what you mean.'

He lowered the field glasses he was holding and passed them over to Kintyre.

'Looks more like a fort than a convent, Major,' said the Irishman. 'Be awful hard to take.'

'We'll wait until the others join us,' said Vickers. 'Then work out a plan of attack.'

'Better be godawful good,' muttered Yarbro. 'That place looks like a fuckin' fort.'

Vickers lit a cigar and turned to Azul.

The halfbreed was building a small fire, getting coffee ready. He grinned at the Army man.

'You think it's too much?'

Vickers shook his head. 'No. It'll be difficult, but I've come too far to give up now. We'll wait for the others to join us, then plan the attack.'

Azul nodded, and began to pass the coffee round. He felt the same kind of anticipatory excitement that had gripped him at the onset of an Apache raid.

He remembered a time when he had been crouched beneath the cover of a ledge with old Sees-The-Fox, waiting until they were sure a whole full bunch of Mexican horses were inside the corral. The Mexicans had raided the ponies from a series of American ranches, picking up Apache mustangs along the way. Killing two warriors and one woman as they rode out.

The Chiricahua *rancherias* and those of the Mescalero had joined together to mount a pursuit. And deep into Mexico, Azul had asked Sees-The-Fox a question.

There are many of them, he had said, *and they all carry the fast-firing guns. All we have is ten warriors with bows. Suppose they shoot us?*

That does not matter, Sees-The-Fox had said. *We have honour to defend. Besides, they do not know how we fight to keep what is ours. How we fight to keep our honour. If they had known that, they would never have dared to steal our ponies.*

They had gone on in at dawn and killed the Mexican rustlers, taking back the horses that belonged to the Apache and dividing the others up amongst them. For his part, Azul had been granted two fine mares. He was seventeen then.

Around noon the other groups of Army men came in.

Slowly, in scattered bunches, just like Azul had planned: so they wouldn't attract too much attention.

They camped out over night, and while the dawn was still spreading a roseate colour through the mist, took their orders and went down to carry them out.

Twenty men were detailed off under the command of a captain called Sobel to take seizure of Santa Rosa. The remaining ten went off with Azul and Vickers to skirt around the town and approach the convent from the south. It was agreed that they would follow an altered version of the halfbreed's savagely simple plan: Sobel was to enter the town and capture Aranjuez, then – with the fat mayor his prisoner – he was to approach the convent from the front. Azul, meanwhile, would lead Vickers and his party to the rear. If Aranjuez was unable to persuade the bandits to open the gates, then Sobel would mount a frontal assault while commanding the trail up from Santa Rosa and thus cutting off reinforcements. Azul and Vickers would attempt a sortie from behind. It was all totally illegal, a breach of international border agreements, and the kind of action that would see every soldier before a court martial if it failed. And if they lived that long. And every man knew it; and not one cared. Following the raids and the slaughter of the troopers at the river, they were determined to extract revenge. It was the kind of feeling Azul could understand.

Captain Martin Sobel was twenty-seven years old, and ambitious. He knew he was on a make-or-break mission with only three possible results: death, dishonour or glory – which should lead to promotion. He grinned tightly as he gave his orders and began to descend the slope.

The sun was not yet out, a grey bank of low cloud cover hanging over the valley, extending tendrils over the upper slopes so that the convent was hidden from view. Santa Rosa was not yet awake.

Sobel's men broke into separate groups as they entered the town, spacing themselves around the central plaza so that they covered the cantinas and sidestreets while the captain and five picked men approached the building Azul had pointed out.

They hitched their horses to the rail outside and climbed the stoop. The *alcalde's* house was imposing, two storeys high with wide, wrought iron-covered windows either side of a massive double door. A balcony ran along the frontage above the door, a Mexican flag hanging limp from its white-painted pole. Sobel drew his Colt's Cavalry model and clicked the hammer back. The sound seemed to ring unnaturally loud in the early morning stillness. He hammered on the woodwork.

No sound came from the interior. The captain hammered again and a voice growled irritably, followed by the slap of *huaraches* on tiles. Then bolts creaked and the doors shifted slightly open. Sobel rammed a shoulder against one side, a trooper crashed against the other.

An old man cried out as the doors swung open and the Americans went through, staggering back under the impact of the in-flung wood. The troopers moved with precision, fanning out in a semi-circle beyond the door, Springfields covering the staircase and the openings off the hall. Sobel grabbed the old man by the front of his shirt and jammed the Colt up against his cheek.

'Where's Aranjuez?'

The old man shook his head, veined eyes flickering panic-stricken from side to side.

Sobel switched to Spanish, '*Dónde está Aranjuez? Rápido!*'

'There.' The terrified old man pointed up the stairs. 'The second room.'

Sobel held the hammer back as he swung the Colt against the oldster's skull. The barrel landed along the temple and for an instant the Mexican's eyes rounded wide. Then they snapped shut as his body went limp. Sobel let him fall to the floor, snapping orders as he crossed the room.

'Mullion, watch the door. Callan and Waites, you hold this room. The rest stay with me.'

He took the stairs at a run, ignoring the clatter of his metalled Cavalry boots on the polished wood, counting on speed to carry him through. Before very long the citizens of Santa Rosa would know something was wrong anyway, and by then he wanted the *alcalde* securely under guard.

He reached the head of the stairs and was turning to the door the old man had indicated when a sleepy-eyed *pistolero* stepped onto the balcony. The man was barefoot and naked from the waist up. He was holding an ornately-chased S & W Schofield in his right hand, and still yawning. The trooper behind Sobel drove his carbine forwards like a rapier, the muzzle driving deep into the Mexican's hairy belly. The *pistolero* grunted and doubled over, letting go the pistol. The trooper jerked his carbine back and took hold of the forepart, swinging the stock up in a vicious arc that slammed the edge hard against the man's chin. Teeth splintered and a thin trickle of blood ran down over the beard stubble as the *pistolero* slumped unconscious.

Sobel grabbed the doorhandle and turned it. The lock clicked open and the door swung inwards. The captain, followed by the two privates, charged into the room.

It was luxurious. Thick carpets covered the floor and heavy drapes reduced the light to a gloomy dimness. There was a table at the centre, its carved wood matching the decorations covering the big wardrobe and the dressing-table. There was a smell of perfume and lavender water and pomade, mingling with the ranker odour of sweat. On the far side, facing the mirror of the dressing-table, there was an enormous bed. The sheets were rumpled, and in the dim light it was hard to see if it was occupied. Sobel held his gun pointed at the pillows as he snatched back the drapes.

The light of early dawn paled into the room and from the centre of the bed a moustachioed face appeared.

'*Qué es?*' demanded Luis Felipe de Aranjuez irritably. Then gasped as he saw the three men.

His gasp was echoed twice by the two women who emerged from the tangled sheets beside him. Both were young – no more than twenty – with tousled hair and sleep-filled eyes. Their lips were swollen and bite marks showed on their breasts.

'Christ!' muttered a trooper.

Sobel grabbed a handful of sheet and yanked the whole lot clear of the bed. The girls squealed and began to untangle their entwined limbs. Aranjuez spluttered and dropped his hands to cover himself.

'Out!' snapped Sobel. 'Get dressed.'

Aranjuez stared at the Colt and changed his mind about arguing. His flabby belly trembled as he scurried across the floor to the wardrobe. Sobel went with him, keeping the handgun close to the plump Mexican's face as the mayor hurried into his clothes. Without turning, he said, 'Hopper, keep watching that goddam door. Leave the women to Atkins.'

'Yessir!' came the answer. Echoed with more relish by Atkins.

'Who are you?' Aranjuez gained courage with his clothing. 'You'll never get away with this.'

'Shut up!' snarled Sobel. 'Just do exactly what I tell you.'

'Visitors,' called Hopper. 'Armed.'

Sobel grabbed Aranjuez and spun him round. By now the mayor was wearing pants and a shirt. He had his boots on. The captain grabbed the back of his collar and marched him to the door. The Colt was jammed hard into the small of the Mexican's back.

'Tell them to drop their guns.'

'They'll kill you,' said Aranjuez.

Sobel twisted the Colt so that the foresight snagged on the folds of loose flesh, twisting them cruelly. Aranjuez groaned.

'You won't live to see it,' grated Sobel. 'Tell them!'

'Drop your guns!' Tears of rage and pain filled the fat man's eyes. 'Do what this *gringo* tells you.'

Three pistols thudded to the floor. Three *pistoleros* stood gaping at their *jefe*.

'We're goin' out,' said Sobel; flat and cold. 'Anyone tries to stop us, Aranjuez dies first.'

'Get back. For God's sake, get back!' Fear rendered the Mexican's voice harsh. 'Don't try anything.'

Sobel pushed him out of the room, flanked by the two troopers. They moved past the Mexicans, pausing just long enough to snatch up their guns before descending the stairs. In the room below, Callan and Waites were holding their carbines on a group of servants, and Mullion was watching the plaza.

He turned as he heard Sobel come down the stairs. 'Crowd buildin', captain. They look ugly.'

Sobel frog-marched Aranjuez to the door and peered out. Twenty or thirty people were clustered around the plaza, watching the soldiers like wolves estimating their chances of a successful attack; and like wolves, waiting for a leader to show them the way. Sobel stepped onto the porch. A low, ugly murmur went up.

'Tell 'em.' The captain prodded Aranjuez with the Colt. 'Make it good.'

Aranjuez began to speak. His voice was high-pitched, squeaky, the words carrying shrill through the silence that had fallen. When he was finished the silence continued. In a way, it was more ominous than any violent reaction.

'All right!' Sobel yelled. 'Mount up.'

The troopers mounted, still holding their guns pointed on the crowd. Sobel issued more orders and Aranjuez was lifted onto Hopper's horse, his ankles lashed to the stirrups, his wrists to the pommel. Hopper climbed up behind Atkins, then Sobel swung astride his own mount. He looped a rope around Aranjuez's neck and fixed the end to his own saddle.

'Nice an' easy,' he said. 'Up the hill.'

'The Sisters?' The fat Mexican ignored the rope as he turned to stare in disbelief at the officer. 'You're crazy.'

'Maybe,' grunted Sobel, 'but that's where we're going. Now move!'

They rode down through Santa Rosa in a tight, slow-moving group, eyeing the watchful citizens all the way. The sun was up now, breaking the cloud cover so that a cool-looking, grey-blue sky showed through. High above them the sun shone on the forbidding walls of the convent, shining a treacherously virginal white. They crossed the bridge spanning the river, hooves clattering loud on the boards, and went on past the low-built warehouses and the smaller buildings that marked the outskirts of Santa Rosa. Sobel held his gun rock-steady on Aranjuez's back all the way.

'We done it.' Mullion let out a low whistle. 'We goddam done it.'

'Only half, Sergeant.' Sobel looked up at the blocky walls above them. 'The hard part's yet to come.'

'Jesus!' Vickers spat the stub of his cigar onto the ground and mashed it into the earth. 'It looks even worse from close up.'

'I never said it was easy,' grinned Azul.

'No.' Vickers acknowledged the statement with a nod. 'But you sure made it sound possible.'

Azul shrugged. 'You've come too far to back out now, Major.'

'I guess.' The Army man looked at the halfbreed with a contemplative stare. 'You plan all this because of what they did to you?'

Azul shrugged without replying.

'Jesus Christ!' murmured Vickers. 'I think you did. I honest to God think you talked me into using the U.S. Army to fight your battle.'

Azul just smiled and checked his guns.

They were crouched inside the gulley behind the rear walls, the overhanging lip hiding them from view. While Sobel had been busy taking Aranjuez, they had worked

84

round to the ridge and gone down on ropes while the sky was still misty. Now they waited for the gates to open, or the firing to begin.

A trooper came down the gulley, moving on all fours.

'Captain Sobel's on his way up, sir. Got a fat Mex with big moustaches out front.'

'Aranjuez,' grunted Azul. 'He must've pulled it off.'

'I hope we can manage the rest,' said Vickers, then turned to the private. 'How long before he reaches that plateau, soldier?'

'He's moving slow, sir. I'd reckon thirty minutes, maybe longer.'

Vickers nodded and dismissed the man. He combed his fingers through his beard as his grey eyes fastened again on Azul's face.

'I was right the first time around,' he muttered. 'You're a real mean bastard.'

'Only on the first count,' Azul grinned. 'My folks were married.'

CHAPTER TEN

Clear of Santa Rosa, Sobel took the rope from Aranjuez's neck. The trail was sided steeply enough that the fat Mexican had nowhere to run except forwards, and he was reminded that he couldn't outpace a bullet.

'What do you want me to do?' he whined. 'They won't open the gates.'

'You tell 'em we're real mean *yanqui* gunhands,' said Sobel. 'Say we heard about this place from a halfbreed we killed, an' now we want in. We want to join them.'

'*Madre de Dios*!' Aranjuez shook his head. 'Even if they believe me, they won't agree. They'll shoot you down.'

'That'll be tough on you,' said Sobel. 'Because you'll be right between us.'

He motioned for the Mexican to go on climbing.

It was shortly after noonday, the sun almost directly overhead. The cloud was all broken up now, the air warm with the midday heat of late Autumn. Sobel hoped he had timed it right : so that the bandits would be eating, or starting their siesta. Below the final crest he called a halt, issuing his last orders. Sergeant Mullion, Waites, Hopper and Atkins would approach the gates with him and Aranjuez in the lead; the rest would stay under cover until they heard firing. Then they were to come up fast. At the same time, Vickers and his men would be attacking from the rear.

'I hope it works,' murmured the sergeant, adding a *sir* as an afterthought.

'So do I,' answered Sobel. 'Let's go.'

They moved up the final stretch, cresting the rimrock with Aranjuez in front, and came onto the plateau. Sobel breathed a low, slow sigh when he saw the gates were open. Not all the way, but enough that two horses might pass through side-by-side. There was a man lounging just inside the opening, too busy lighting a cheroot to spot the riders before they were out onto the bare flat. When he saw them, he dropped his cheroot and picked up the Winchester canted at his feet. The captain glanced up at the watchtowers, grateful for the fact that they were empty. The Mexican called something through the gates and a second man came out, chewing a taco and holding a Henry repeater. Sobel went on riding, close behind Aranjuez.

'*Don* Luis?' the man with the cheroot sounded surprised. 'What do you want?'

'Visitors!' Aranjuez fought to hold his voice under control, horribly conscious of the two rifles pointing at his chest and Sobel's handgun behind him. 'They are outlaws from across the Border. They say they heard about the Sisters from a man they killed. The halfbreed.'

'Keep moving,' urged Sobel as the Mexican slowed his horse. 'Get up close.'

'The halfbreed?' The guard sounded surprised. 'He must be dead by now. We left him on the cross.'

'He got away.' Sobel spoke as the fat mayor's voice dried completely. 'We ran across him an' he told us about this place. We want in.'

The guards exchanged glances. By now Sobel and his men were within a few yards of the gates. 'Wait,' ordered one. 'Jose must decide this.' He turned to his companion, muttering something too low for Sobel to hear.

As he turned, Sobel sprang into action. He lifted his Colt, arm extended straight out over his horse's neck, and drove his heels hard against the animal's flanks. Cavalry trained, the horse charged forwards, ignoring the shot that blasted close by its head. The Mexicans swung round, lifting their rifles in clumsy surprise. Sobel's bullet hit the man who had been chewing the taco. It tore into the front of his grease-stained shirt, slightly below his right shoulder so that he was spun round and back, his mouth gaping to emit morsels of half-chewed food. His hand flew loose of the Henry's trigger and then he dropped the gun as he crashed against the left-side gate. He crumpled to a sitting position, staring stupidly at the crimson staining the side of his body.

His companion reacted faster. The Winchester came up to his shoulder as he shuffled backwards through the gates, his mouth opening to shout a warning. By then, Sobel – with Mullion and the others close behind – was at the opening. The captain was blasting shots ahead of his charge and the troopers were laying down random fire in through the gates. The Mexican loosed off a single shot before three bullets caught him, lifting him off his feet as red blossomed across his chest and a massive hole appeared in his neck, sending a spray of bright scarlet arcing into the convent. The .44–40 slug missed the Americans: Aranjuez was not so lucky.

Don Luis Felipe de Aranjuez, *alcalde* of Santa Rosa, owner of numerous farms and landlord of two cantinas, was screaming in fear. Sobel's sudden move had taken him completely by surprise. The first inkling he got was the blast of the captain's gun and the abrupt charge. The horse he was riding was a Cavalry mount: it followed its companions in the rush for the gates, and the fat little mayor – lashed firmly to the saddle – was unable to control it. Consequently he was carried straight into the path of the guard's bullet.

The shot hit his sternum, splintering the bone to deflect off to the right side. The force of it rocked Aranjuez back in the saddle hard enough that his horse screamed and began to paw air. The shock numbed out the agony of the secondary wounding as the bullet ploughed between his ribs to penetrate a lung. Aranjuez was dimly aware of something warm flowing from his mouth as he screamed, then a curious lassitude gripped him and he slumped over in the saddle. His shifting weight brought the rearing horse crashing down on its side. Aranjuez's left leg crushed between the hard stone of the plateau and the hard edges of the McLellan saddle, femur, tibia and fibula all shattering so that spikey shards of bone ripped through the flesh. The fresh wounding broke through the numbing effects of the first shock, and his lips opened to emit a huge, howling yell that bubbled to an end as his mouth and throat filled with blood and he began to choke. The horse, panicked now, struggled to regain its feet. The weight of the rider made it impossible, and the creature thrashed back over, half-rolling onto Aranjuez. The pelvic girdle splintered, fragments of bone driving upwards into the entrails, then the cantle edged down against the man's belly. The flesh gave under the horse's weight, tearing so that a massive rupture emptied a flood of stinking yellow intestines over the ground as the sac of the stomach burst. Aranjuez saw one last glimpse of sky before it was blotted out behind a curtain of red that thundered over his vision, then transformed everything to blackness.

The horse struggled to its feet and began to trot nervously around the plateau. Draped along its side was the ragdoll that had once been Luis Felipe de Aranjuez.

Up at the gates Sobel was crouched behind the body of his horse, trading fire with the bandits grouped on the far side of the interior court. Mullion was ignoring the bullets spattering around his head as he drove his own mount against the other gate, forcing it steadily back while Hopper, Waites and Atkins gave him covering fire. He got the gate all the way open and was yelling for the rest of the attackers to come on in when a shot hit his jaw and stopped his voice for ever. It struck the right side, fragmenting the bone so that his whole jawline was smashed abruptly out of line. Broken teeth imbedded in his cheeks and half his tongue fell away into the crimson wash that covered his chest. A bullet took his mount in the skull and it dropped like a poleaxed steer. Mullion tumbled to the ground, left hand reaching up to touch his face. It came away sticky with blood, and the big sergeant uttered one gut-wrenching scream before lifting to his feet to charge headlong across the courtyard with his Colt blazing flame in front.

Behind him, the attackers ceased their fire as his wavering charge took him over their line of sight. The bandits fired in a volley. Mullion's body was picked up and hurled back. Spurts of red erupted from his chest and stomach and face. His arms flailed wildly, the hammer of the Colt still clicking on empty cylinders. Then he hit the ground and lay still, scarlet pulsing from his curiously deflated corpse.

'For Chrissakes!' yelled Sobel. 'Keep 'em away from

those goddam towers. Don't let 'em get above us.'

The remainder of his men came running up to the gates, and they began to move inside.

'They're in position, said Vickers. 'Let's go.'

Azul grabbed a rope and began to haul himself up the side of the convent. There was a single shot. From a pistol. Followed close by an emptying cylinder and the bark of a single rifle. He was three-quarters up the wall when a volley of pistol shots rang out, then silence as he made the last few feet to the top.

Men were shouting from inside the walls, and the silence got broken by the concentrated blast of gunfire. He clambered over the parapet and looked down. The bandits were spilling out of the big central building, Jose Cabra in the lead, too far away for the handgun to travel. Captain Sobel was down inside one gate, his dead horse jamming the wood open. A sergeant was struggling to force the other, and three troopers were doing their best to cover his suicidal attempt. One was sprawled on his face with the back of his skull wide open.

Azul turned, reaching down to haul Vickers over the lip.

'Ladders,' he shouted over the firing, pointing at the wooden structures running down to the ground. Vickers nodded and yelled for his men to follow him without waiting for the last few to climb the ropes.

They skidded down the ladders, landing at the rear of the convent where three big wagons were lined up. A woman Azul didn't recognise came out of the central building with bandoliers draped over her shoulders. She had red hair. The halfbreed shot her without thinking, spilling her body backwards across the entrance. Someone grabbed her arms as he moved out of cover and raced across the courtyard, hauling her back inside the room. Someone else began to fire a pistol from a window.

Azul dropped to the ground, finding refuge behind a low wall that encircled a flowerbed. Vickers fell beside him.

'Thirty men,' the major bellowed. 'Better armed. Fire on my order.'

The Mexicans were grouped along one wall of the building, sheltered by the well and a parked wagon. Cabra was shouting something, gesturing furiously. A bandolier flew through the air, tossed from a window Azul couldn't see, and the Mexican scooped it up, ducking down as he began to reload.

'Now!' Vickers commanded.

The troopers came up from behind the sheltering wall, firing military-style, left elbow on raised left knee, left hand cupping the butt. Their volley took the bandits by surprise, confusing the whole issue as Mexicans went down with red blossoming from their backs. Cabra turned and threw himself flat as the second volley rang out. He rolled across the open space, fetching up close against the wall of the big central edifice so that he was sheltered on both sides. His men were slower to react. Some continued to trade fire with Sobel's force as it spilled in through the gates, while others began to fire in Azul's direction.

The halfbreed saw the giant with the ringlets turn and gape straight at him. And fired once.

The bullet hit the man in his open mouth. It ripped into the soft flesh at the back and tore through to exit from the rear of the giant's neck in a great fountain of scarlet. The wound would have downed a smaller man, but the gigantic Mexican shook his head, spraying droplets of blood in a fan about him and lumbered to his feet, triggering his Remington. Azul shot him in the belly. Low down, where the man had kicked him. The giant tottered, stooping slightly as the front of his dark blue pants turned crimson. Then he fell down as the halfbreed aimed and planted a slug through his left knee. His leg twisted, shifting out from under him at an unnatural angle, and he pitched forwards onto his face. His hair was plastered stickily to the back of his neck, and as he pushed up on his hands, great wellings of blood gouted down his back. Azul sighted and fired again. The giant was staring at him, recognition filling his piggy eyes with luminous hate. The fourth bullet hit exactly midway between the eyes, dulling the luminosity as it shattered bone and plunged into the soft substance of his brain. It destroyed the lower

part, ricochetting off the inside of his skull to smash outwards through the top. The giant's head jerked back as
sticky grey brain matter and fragments of white bone
gouted upwards through his hair. His arms flung out
rigid, and for a moment he knelt upright as though
exposing his wounds. Then, like some massive tree falling,
he toppled forwards, the hole in his skull like an accusing
eye fixed on the halfbreed.

Azul fired his last bullet at a Mexican running for the
shelter of the building and began to reload.

Sobel and his men were moving round the inside of the
walls now, spreading out to catch the last of the bandits
still in the open in a cross-fire. The air was thick with the
reek of spent powder : loud with the screaming of dying
men. Gradually the shooting lessened, until the only
defensive fire came from inside the central building.

'They're trapped!' Vickers rasped. 'We got the bastards
cornered.'

'There's Santa Rosa,' Azul reminded. 'The town could
send men up.'

The Army officer nodded. 'Yeah, but Sobel's left men
there. Five can hold that trail now we got the high
ground.' He looked at the building sheltering the sur-
vivors.

It was like a block-house. The walls were pocked with
bullet holes, showing solid stone under the adobe plaster-
ing. The doors were closed and the shutters over the
windows were down, rifles angling from the firing ports.

'What's it like inside?'

Azul shrugged. 'They didn't take me on a tour. Strong,
I guess. Like a mission house.' He wracked his mind for
some distinct memory of the interior. 'There were rooms
at the sides. A big room at the centre. That's all I know.'

'Hearth?' asked Vickers. 'A fireplace of some kind?'

'Must be,' the halfbreed nodded, understanding. 'I'll
check it.'

Without waiting for a reply he turned and darted
across the courtyard. A few random shots echoed after
him, but he reached the outer wall safely and climbed a
ladder to the catwalk. From there, he could see the roof
of the block-house. It was built up around the edges,

drainage gutters running along four sides below a low-sloped apex of tile. There was a shallow arch at the front end with a cross-bar that had once probably supported a bell. At the farther end there was a similar structure. He ran along the catwalk, circling the walls until he could look down on the rear. There was another arch, as he had suspected, but this one had no cross-bar. Instead, there was a tiled cone above a wide, circular hole. The stonework of the arch was blackened, the cone thick with soot. He smiled; a cold, ugly expression; and went back to Vickers.

The major was talking with Sobel.

'All right,' he was saying, 'we lost eight men. We got them bottled up now, though. And that goddam storehouse must hold everything they took from over the river. Now we gotta get them out.'

'And get back,' added the captain. 'That may not be easy.'

'We'll make it,' said Vickers confidently.

Sobel began to say something else, but Azul interrupted him.

'Chimney at the rear,' he rasped. 'We can smoke them out.'

Vickers nodded. 'Good. Let's start.'

The stables and store sheds provided ample quantities of inflammable material: hay, oil, tarpaulins. There was ammunition stacked in one outbuilding, and kegs of black powder. Sobel was detailed off to supervise the gathering.

'Now we got just one more problem,' he said when it was all ready. 'How do we get close to the roof?'

He gestured at the walls of the block-house, where rifles were still spitting flame from the gunports. The building stood separate from the others, surrounded on all four sides by open space. There was no way a man could get close without coming under a murderous crossfire from the windows.

'Fight fire with fire,' Azul grated. 'Give me some men and I'll show you.'

Vickers nodded and detailed off six troopers.

Azul took them over to the parked wagons and selected

one of the largest, a high-sided vehicle that looked like it might have been the one he escorted from Ysabel. He helped the soldiers pile hay into the back, then doused the load with oil. At his command they turned the wagon around and began to manhandle the thing past the storehouses until it was lined on the alley running between the block-house and the walls. Then he fastened ropes to the forward axle, passing the double line out to the troopers as he explained his plan. A third line was fixed to the brake.

When he gave the order, they all began to push. The wagon moved slowly down the alley, gradually picking up speed. Shots drummed against the side and rear as it rolled clear of the last storehouse and entered the killing ground around the central building. The troopers let it go, the ropes snaking between their hands. When Azul shouted, they grabbed hold of the lines and braced their weight against the momentum of the vehicle. Azul held the third line, calculating the distance. He shouted again, and the soldiers dug their heels in as the halfbreed snatched back the line connected to the brake. The wagon slowed, then ground to a halt. It was close against the rear of the block-house.

Azul picked up a lantern, turning the wick high and smashing the glass funnel. He lit the wick. Then he hurled the lantern in an arc across the intervening space.

It landed on the wagon, kerosene spilling from the tank so that a sheet of pale yellow flame lifted above the oil-soaked hay. Abruptly, the oil took fire. Darker flames blotted out the light of the kerosene, then got lost themselves in the tendrils of smoke writhing thick and black from the hay. Heat began to blister the adobe, dark fingers of soot climbing up the walls of the building until they, in turn, were obscured behind the roiling clouds of stinking smoke.

Azul led his squad back to the pile of inflammable material and picked out what he needed. Then he took them up one of the ladders to the catwalk and ran round to a point overlooking the blazing wagon. The firing from this side had ceased : the oily hay was blotting out all vision so that the whole rear end of the block-house was lost behind the pall of smoke. The halfbreed looked down from his vantage point, barely able to make out the squat shape of the chimney as he unshipped a rope and began to whirl the noose about his head.

It took him four attempts before he caught a loop over the stone and lashed the other end to the crenellations of the wall. The rope went down at an angle, slanting from the catwalk to the roof of the block-house. Azul grasped it in both hands and dropped away. Behind him, he heard a soldier mutter : 'Christ ! he'll fry.'

He began to haul himself hand-over-hand along the rope, moving steadily – aided by the slant – towards the fire. Smoke roiled about his face and he felt the soles of his moccasins scorch. He swung his legs up, hooking both feet over the rope and let himself slide the last part.

He entered a stinking darkness that watered his eyes and filled his nostrils with foul-smelling vapours. Flame seared his back, and he was grateful for the protction of his leather vest. Then he felt the wall hot against his hands and twisted round to seize the parapet. The heat was intense, and he dragged himself over the lip of the roof as swiftly as his precarious hold allowed. He fell onto the flat part of the roof, choking and blinking his smoke-filled eyes furiously. As he rested there, the rope parted, falling away in a thin trail of sparks. He stood up.

When he shouted, a bundle came flying through the smoke. He grabbed it and tossed it to the side, away from the heated part of the wall.

Another shout brought a second bundle. Then two more : he was ready.

He began to unwrap the bundles, rolled in squares of tarpaulin to protect them from the heat, setting them out on the flat of the roof. When he was finished he used his Bowie to pierce the small keg of oil and poured the contents down the chimney. Then he emptied a box of .44-40 cartridges after it, and followed that with the tank of a kerosene lantern. Next, he took a second lantern and lit the wick. Then dropped it after the other. There was a *whooshing* sound from the chimney, like a sudden gust of wind rushing down a narrow canyon, and a needle of flame spurted upwards through the smoke.

Azul grabbed the squares of tarpaulin and stuffed them into the hole, ignoring the heat and the singeing hairs on his arms and hands. Faintly through the muffling effects of the canvas he could hear the crackle of exploding shells from inside the building.

He moved around the roof to the front. Immediately below him was the big double door, flanked either side by gunports. He could see Vickers and Sobel watching him from the cover of an overturned wagon, shouting something he couldn't hear through the crackle of gunfire.

He pointed down at the door, then at the inflammables piled against the far wall. Vickers understood, waving an answer. The halfbreed nodded his reply and swung his legs over the parapet. He slid off, twisting to catch the edge of the stone with both hands, his toes banging against the reinforced wood of the doors. He hung there for a moment, knowing that he must calculate his drop exactly, or roll out to where the defenders might kill him.

He let go.

As he struck the hard ground fronting the doors, he bent his knees, absorbing the shock with the powerful muscles of his thighs and calves, dropping his arms to cover his face. He ignored the shock of the landing, straightening his legs so that he was thrown forwards against the woodwork of the doors, instead of rolling back. His arms stung from the impact, his spread palms numbing as they hit the metal studs covering the surface. But he was standing upright, flattened against the doors.

He turned round, shouting at Vickers.

The major shouted back and a burly corporal sprang up from behind the wagon with a keg lifting in his arms. It curled through the air, thrown with sufficient accuracy that it landed neatly in Azul's outflung hands. The halfbreed staggered under the impact, almost toppling forwards before he righted himself and settled the keg between his feet. The corporal tossed another over, this time encircled with a length of grey cord.

Azul used the Bowie again to pierce both kegs, the splintering wood giving off a spray of black powder. He unwound the fuse from the second keg and measured off two slightly unequal lengths. Then he stuffed the ends into each keg and set them against the doors, close to the centre. He lit the fuses, the longest first, and dropped flat on the ground.

The fuses sizzled as he crawled below the line of the nearest gunport, moving fast around the corner of the building until he was flattened against the wall, halfway down.

Vickers' men ceased firing on that side. Then everyone stopped. There was a moment of ominous stillness, like the calm preceding a bad storm.

And the two kegs of powder exploded.

There was a terrific roar. A tremor ran down the wall. Then chunks of wood rained in all directions, followed by a shout from the soldiers.

Azul moved back to the front of the block-house as Vickers brought his men forwards. Both doors were hanging at crazy angles, the lower hinges blasted away along with the lock and the crossbar. The wood smouldered, jagged-edged gaps showing where the main brunt of the explosion had landed. The troopers kicked the doors in and stormed through.

Inside, there was carnage. The entire central room was thick with smoke. Pieces of flesh were spread in a swathe from the doors. Bodies lay still and bleeding. A handful of Mexicans were still on their feet, shaking their heads and coughing as they raised their hands in surrender. More were stretched on the floor, clutching at wounds and groaning as they saw the Army men rush in.

Azul recognised the body of the woman he had known as Sister Maria crumpled by the hearth. An exploding cartridge had penetrated her face, entering below the left cheekbone to exit through the socket of her right eye. It looked almost as though she was winking at him. He left her where she lay, moving with Vickers' men into the side rooms.

The force of the explosion had not penetrated here, nor the full effect of the blocked chimney: there was some resistance.

It came from both the Mexican bandits and the

women. Not very much, because there were too few left alive. But for a short time it was bitter, room-to-room fighting.

Azul kicked a door open and saw the fat bandit who had been with Cabra that first time crouched behind an overturned table. The Mexican was holding the S & W Russian in his left hand. His right was shattered. His bullets flew wild, and the halfbreed ducked around the edge of the door to plant two slugs in the sweating, frightened face. One blasted the Mexican's left eye to pulp, travelling on into his brain so that he jerked back and upright as it exited from the base of his skull. The second impounded the injury as it smashed the bone just above the eye and enlarged the socket to an enormous hole that gaped stickily red from the man's face. It exploded from his skull in a great welter of crimson that was flecked through with shards of bone and pieces of brain matter. He crashed back against the wall, leaving a wide, crimson smear where he landed, and slid wetly down until he sprawled on the floor, staring one-eyed across the room.

A woman screamed, and the halfbreed dropped as a small-calibre pistol spat flame. Unthinking, acting on pure reflex, he fired in the direction of the shot.

And saw Julia lifted off her feet by the impact of the .45 calibre slug that had gone in between her ample breasts. She was wearing a pale blue dress that emphasised the brightness of the blood pulsing from her cleavage. The dress ruckled up as she struck the wall and bounced off to land heavily on the floor. She was wearing black stockings and a scarlet suspender belt that matched the colour of her blood. Her blonde hair was darkened by smoke, and her face was pale and furious. She moaned something inarticulate as she lifted the little derringer and took careful aim at the halfbreed.

Azul fired again. The slug hit the underside of the woman's left breast, entering the heart and smashing the vital organ before glancing off a rib to lodge against her spine. The derringer lifted out of line under the impact, expending its slug into the ceiling. Julia was dead before it landed.

'Christ! You coulda given the woman a chance.'

Azul turned to the soldier behind him. He was young, no more than twenty, and his face was pale as Julia's.

'I seen her use her weapon,' he rasped. 'She knew how to handle it.'

'Yeah, but you coulda warned her. Or something . . .'

The trooper's voice tailed off as the halfbreed glanced at him. There was an instant, when their eyes met, that he knew he was looking at death. That if he went on talking – saying the wrong thing – he, too, might go down under the halfbreed's rage. He let his eyes drop, shaking his head.

Later, when he got a chance to discuss it all, he told his friends about the incident. Having seen Azul in action, they agreed that the halfbreed was a bad man to cross. 'Funny thing is,' said one, 'I don't think he gave a damn about them *bandidos* stealin' American money, or killin' folks. I reckon all he wanted to do was even his own score. So he used us to do it.' The others nodded, agreeing.

The block-house was starting to burn. Not badly yet, but enough that the fires started by the explosion and the muffled chimney could bring it down in a while. Vickers had grouped his prisoners in the courtyard outside. There were ten women and six bandits.

When Azul checked them over he saw no sign of Jose Cabra, Linda, or Teresa.

'So they got killed,' said Vickers. 'They're inside.'

'No.' Azul shook his head. 'I looked at the bodies.'

'No-one got out,' frowned Vickers. 'What you think they done? Dug their way out?'

Azul remembered something about old Spanish missions and nodded. 'Maybe. Let me talk to one of the prisoners. Alone.'

The officer shrugged. 'All right. I'm gonna hang the men, anyway. But how can it help you?'

'Maybe I can get to the bottom of the thing,' said the halfbreed; flat and ugly.

CHAPTER ELEVEN

The shed was empty. The walls were blank adobe, featureless except where two small windows set high up on either side filtered light in. The door was closed, barred on the outside and watched by two soldiers. The floor was packed dirt.

The Mexican stood warily at the farther end.

'Tell me,' said Azul, almost casually. 'Tell me how they got away.'

'I don't know how.' The man stared at the halfbreed, his face contorted midway between hatred and fear. 'Maybe they were killed.'

Azul shook his head. 'They weren't. I checked the bodies. All of them. Cabra and the two women got away.'

'I don't know,' shrugged the bandit. 'Why ask me?'

'You're not wounded,' said Azul slowly, letting the words sink in. 'A wounded man dies faster.'

'I don't know,' the Mexican repeated.

'They left you,' said Azul. 'They left you to hold off the *yanquis* while they escaped.'

The man shrugged again, not answering.

'All right,' said Azul. 'You chose the way.'

He drew the Bowie knife, stroking the edge with his thumb. Light caught the blade, sending shimmering reflections over the walls, over the man's face. The Mexican crouched. Azul moved slowly forwards down the centre of the narrow room.

The Mexican shifted to the side, looking at the door. Azul moved to block him. He stepped forward, the knife drooping from his right hand, cutting edge uppermost. The Mexican crossed the room. It took him three sideways steps. Azul pivoted, again blocking his path. Abruptly, the bandit voiced a low cry and hurled himself forwards, hands outstretched, clawed. It was a move of desperation.

Azul sidestepped, avoiding the clutching arms as he thrust out his left foot to trip the man. At the same time he pivoted, slashing the Bowie across the ribs. The Mexican's shirt parted on two thin lips of blood. The bandit winced, going down on his face. Azul waited until he got back on his feet.

'You'll tell me in the end,' he murmured; confident. 'Make it easy.'

The Mexican pressed his right hand to his side, bringing it away to stare at the crimson on his palm.

'Bastard,' he said slowly. 'Halfbreed bastard.'

Azul said nothing. Just moved towards the man with his right arm lifting up and out, flicking twice – very fast – on a horizontal line that swung from right to left and back again.

The bandit gasped, looking down at the tattered front of his shirt. At the two deep cuts across his chest.

'Tell me,' Azul repeated.

And again the man shook his head.

The halfbreed moved even faster than before. He stepped in close before the Mexican knew what was happening and worked the knife in a criss-cross pattern, the shine of the blade getting lost under the sudden wash of red. When he stepped away, the man's whole chest was zig-zagged with cuts.

The Mexican went down on his knees. He said, 'Oh, Christ Jesus, please help me.' It wasn't blasphemy.

Azul shifted his grip on the haft, turning the blade so that the cutting edge was now downmost. He raised his arm and dropped it. The Mexican's left ear fell loose, tumbling onto his shoulder, then falling to the ground. Tears burst from his eyes.

'While you can still hear me,' said Azul. 'Where did they go? Tell me while you've still got a tongue.'

He dug the point of the blade into the man's cheek as he said it, twisting it so that it grated against the jawbone. The Mexican jerked away. Then his head bowed and he nodded.

'Jose will kill me.'

'You're going to die, anyway,' murmured Azul. 'Your choice is how. Easy, or my way.'

'There's a tunnel.' The bandit's voice was thick now with despair. 'The room at the back. Where you put the wagon. It's under the floor. It comes out by the river.'

'Who took it?' Azul demanded. 'How many?'

'Jose.' The man was openly weeping now. 'He said he was fetching help from Santa Rosa. Then Linda took the girl down. The rest of us couldn't escape because of that explosion. That and the smoke.'

'Thanks,' said Azul, and went to hammer on the door.

When it opened he stepped out past the gaping soldiers. 'Jesus!' said one. 'He's like an animal.' But Azul didn't hear him because he was running for the blockhouse.

'There's a tunnel,' he yelled at Vickers. 'It comes out somewhere above the river. Cabra got out that way.'

'Take a horse.' Vickers pointed at the building. 'You'll roast in there.'

'I don't know where it comes out,' grated Azul. 'I'll take the chance.'

'You're crazy!' Vickers shouted, but Azul didn't hear him. He was gone into the block-house, pausing only long enough to snatch up a lantern.

Inside the building the air was thick with smoke and the reek of burning flesh. Instinct, rather than sight, guided him to the far end of the room, the blaze that was centred on the hearth acting as a kind of beacon. The heat was intense, though when he located the door and stepped into the rear room, he realised the worst was yet to come. The wagon was still burning outside the windows and the room was a swimming pit of oily smoke that clogged his nostrils and threatened to blind him completely. The wood of the shutters was aflame, and the furniture produced a series of individual fires so that the air was almost unbreathable. For a moment he thought of turning back, but then a beam gave way in the outer hall, crashing down across the floor so that the smoke roiled back from a solid curtain of flame. In that instant he saw a disturbance in the thicker smoke, as though a blast of air had cleared it. It came from a point on his left, close against the northern wall.

He moved towards it, hoping that he had made the right choice.

Up close the smoke cleared a little, swirling and eddying so that a kind of hole was bored through the eye-stinging blackness. At the base there was an opening, a square some three feet by three, beside it a heavy wooden block from which small flames were erupting. Choking, feeling vomit rise in his throat, he staggered to the hole.

There was no other escape route now. And this black pit had to be the entrance to the tunnel. He heard a second beam thunder to the floor as he clambered in, ducking as a wash of heat buffeted over his head.

There were steps cut into the side, slanting steeply down so that he lost his footing as the flame blew over the entrance and licked about his hands. He half-slid, half-fell to the bottom, fetching up on a stone floor that was welcomingly cool. For a while he lay there, sucking in great lungfuls of damp air as he pressed his body against the moist rock. When he could breathe properly again he began to feel around him for the lantern. He found it, and lit it by touch, blinking as the flame grew before his eyes to illuminate the bottom of the pit.

Smoke, sucked in by the cooler air, still curled about him, but at least he could breathe here. See better than above. He moved away from the steps into a natural cavern that had been further enlarged by the original occupants of the convent. It was large, at least twenty feet across, with a low roof from which melting stalactites dripped onto the floor. There were niches cut into the walls, as though the place might once have been a store cellar. Or a crypt. The lantern cast flickering shadows over the walls, and it was not until he had fumbled his way halfway round that he found the exit point.

It looked like all the other niches, perhaps slightly larger, set up from the floor so that the dark interior stared balefully out into the gloom of the main cavern. He could have missed it, except that a faint breeze, an almost imperceptible disturbance of the air, touched his face. And when he thrust the lantern inside, he saw the flame cast shadows down a smooth, round hole that angled slightly downwards. He clambered inside as blazing timber crashed burning shards down the steps behind him, and crawled on hands and knees over the smooth, damp stone.

It was an unpleasant sensation, like crawling into a grave. The walls confined him, brushing against his shoulders in places, and the roof was low enough most of the way that he had to keep his head down, staring at a space a foot before his hands. It crossed his mind that the darkness ahead could hide a gun. And a gun fired inside the tunnel was certain to find its target. But he doubted that Cabra or the women would chance that : more likely they were moving ahead as fast as they could. Which – given the huge bulk of Linda – couldn't be very fast. He went on crawling, feeling like a worm boring its way through an apple. Or a maggot through a corpse.

And after what seemed like an infinity the tunnel opened out into a second cavern.

This was much larger than the first, a great vault of a place, big as a church, with a roof so high he couldn't see it. Phosphorescence glistened ghostly off stalagmites, and the walls were lost in the eerie blackness that spread all around. He halted, stepping away from the lantern in case Cabra was waiting somewhere in the darkness. But there was no sound of movement. No sound of anything. Indeed, the total absence was unnerving. He moved back inside the glow of the lantern, grateful for the light and the faint hiss of the wick. And wondered how he would find the exit from this great vault. There was no discernible trail, the rock too smooth to carry prints of any kind, nor any sign to indicate where the escape route continued. Yet he knew the ultimate exit lay above the river, so presumably it came out somewhere above Santa Rosa. Which should mean a downwards path. He stooped to check the floor. It sloped away from him.

He fetched a cartridge from his belt and dropped it onto the stone. It rolled a little way, then began to spin about the apex of the flanged detonation cap. He picked it up and prised the lead slug loose from the main body. When he dropped that, it rolled straight ahead. He followed it, moving as fast as he could by the faint light.

Several times he stumbled into the weirdly-moulded

shapes of stalagmites, and every so often he had to stop to separate a fresh cartridge when the one he was following got lost in the darkness. The floor of the enormous cavern continued to slope downwards, the incline getting steeper as he penetrated farther into the stygian gloom. And then, as the seventh slug got lost down a gradient even steeper than before, he realised there was a fresh source of light. It glowed off the shapes hanging from the roof, partially a natural luminosity and partly the reflected glow of the lantern. Abruptly he realised that the roof was closing down to meet the floor. He hoped it meant he was close to the exit.

Pressing on, he found himself in a kind of stone forest. A jungle of petrified rock that sprouted limbs both upwards and downwards. The growths were spread dense enough that it was no longer possible to use shells to ascertain the path and he was forced to rely on instinct alone. All around him, the fantastic stone formations gave off an ethereal glow that shone in a myriad colours, like some underground rainbow, flickering and shifting its pattern as he moved onwards. The air was cold and damp, sharp in his smoke-tainted lungs, but soothing to his eyes and the scorched patches of skin. The petrified forest continued all the way to the wall of the cavern, where the stone seemed to drip and slide out to meet the glittering needles. It was blank.

He halted, a sudden feeling of claustrophobia overtaking him as he realised that without the exit passage he could never find his way back through the labyrinth. It was like a dream; or a nightmare. And it brought to his mind a memory of a thing old *Sees-Both-Ways*, the Chiricahua shaman had told him once when they talked of the visions sleep sometimes brings.

A path is easy to follow when you have daylight to guide you, the old man had said, *but not so easy at night. Harder still when there is no moon, or clouds hide the stars. But it is always there. It is the same with dreams. You may not see the path. Sometimes you may think it does not exist, but there is a part of you that knows. You must let that part guide you. Forget your eyes and your ears. Forget all your senses and follow that little piece of*

*your spirit that can show you the way. For there is always
a way, so long as you have the courage of soul to press on.*

'All right,' he spoke to reassure himself, his voice a low
mutter that echoed faintly through the great vault of the
cavern, hissing off the stalagmites and stalagtites, 'so
there's a way. There has to be. Cabra and the women
knew there was a way. Now I have to find it.'

He began to move along the wall of the chamber,
weaving through the stone formations with the lantern
held high in his left hand, where it threw light on the
dripping, encrusted side. That way, he figured, it would
show up any exit passages.

How long it took him, he did not know. Time seemed
meaningless in this strange underworld, but – eventually –
he found it. There was an opening like a gaping mouth,
round-lipped and fanged with pointed, shining teeth. And
when he peered at it, he saw that several of the smaller
growths were broken off. He clambered past them into
the tunnel beyond.

Here, the weird rock formations ceased. The walls were
still running with moisture, but smooth, spaced wide
enough apart and roofed high enough, that he was able
to walk upright. The floor angled down, getting steeper as
he moved farther into the subterranean passageway, and
curving to the right at first, then to the left. The curva-
ture was almost his undoing. He was following the
passage along a wide sweep to the right, the floor canted
over so that he guessed he was traversing the flank of the
mountain, when it suddenly dropped away. He felt himself losing balance and pitched over and back, flattening
his forearms and moccasins against a surface too smooth
and slippery to afford a handhold. His left leg floundered
into emptiness, and for a moment he thought he must
spill into whatever hollow lay below him. Then he
stopped, jammed tight against the wall. Cautiously,
moving very slow, he drew his leg back and rolled onto
his belly. He got up on his knees and shifted warily round.
Then, still pressed against the wall, he held the lantern
out.

It shone on a cave so nearly a perfect roundel that it

resembled the inside of an egg. The perfection was marred by a series of steps cut into the side, leading down from the opening in the wall. On the far side, across a floor that curved down and round and up again, there was another flight, climbing to a second hole. The steps were steep, weathered by the moisture that filled the caverns so that the edges were smoothed away like pebbles in a stream. Across the egg-shaped cave, at the foot of the far steps, there was a dark shape. It was still, not moving; not showing any sign of disturbance at the sudden flood of light.

He eased away from the lip, setting one foot on the first step. Cautiously, wary of falling.

It was difficult to go down the smooth-washed stones with the lantern in one hand and his nerves tingling in anticipation of the shape – the *thing* – across the cave, but he made it to the bottom and drew the Colt. The triple *click*! of the hammer going back on full cock echoed like hammer blows in the eerie silence, the sound familiar: reassuring. He crossed the oddly-sloped floor and halted a few feet from the shape.

Up close, with the lantern shedding radiance over the hump, he could see that it was a body dressed in a black robe. A large body. He kicked it. And a high-pitched, childish voice cried out.

'Linda,' he said.

The shape heaved up, exposing the woman's flabby face, even paler now, and streaked with tears. She was wearing a nun's habit, the headpiece pulled low on her forehead so that her bright red hair was hidden. The brilliant lipstick was gone from her mouth, leaving tiny, puckered lips as sallow as her skin.

'Who is it?' She shielded her eyes from the lantern, trying to see past the glow. 'Did you come back?'

'Yeah.' Azul knew she didn't mean him. 'I came back.'

He put the lantern close enough to his own face that she could recognise him. It brought a thin, wavering scream.

'What happened?' He moved around her to the foot of the steps. 'Where's Cabra? Teresa?'

'They left me.' Her voice was feeble as a child's; querulous and tearful. 'I couldn't climb the steps, so they left me.'

'How long?' he asked.

She shrugged, the movement wobbling the folds of her jowels. 'Not long.'

'How far to the river?'

'Not far. They left me. Just because I couldn't climb the steps.'

Azul eased the hammer of the Colt down. Holstered the gun.

'Where they headed?'

'Santa Rosa. There's money stashed there.' Anger flickered briefly in her piggy eyes, abruptly replaced by a calculating look. 'A lot of money. Getaway money.'

'Where?' he asked.

'I'll show you.' It was a child's cunning whine. 'We'll share it. They shouldn't get it. They left me. They said I was too fat to climb the steps. You're strong: you help me climb the steps. Then we'll kill them and share the money.'

'How long before the river?' asked Azul, ignoring her.

'Not long. A few minutes. After the steps. I'll show you the way.'

She started to ease her massive bulk upwards, wheezing with the effort. Azul set a foot on the first stone and climbed above her.

'Help me up?' she asked. 'Help me up the steps?'

Azul began to climb away from her. 'Where's the money hidden?'

'I'll show you.' She managed to get on her feet, porcine eyes glinting in the lantern's light. 'Help me up the steps and I'll show you.'

Azul reached the top and stared down at her. She lifted her arms towards him.

'Please. Help me up the steps.'

'Lady,' he said, his voice unyielding as the stone, 'you got yourself in a hole.'

Her screams echoed behind him as he moved away down the passage.

CHAPTER TWELVE

The tunnel came out on a ridge overlooking Santa Rosa. It was night, and from the position of the moon he calculated it was a few hours before dawn. The river glittered below him and the roofs of the town shone pale. It was very quiet. The trail up to the convent lay to his left, about a quarter mile off. There was no sign of movement.

The halfbreed descended the slope, clambering through the timber that studded the steep gradient at a speed that threatened to spill him headlong to the bottom. He reached the terracing of a hill farm safely and made better time on the surer ground, dropping from one terrace to the next as though bounding down a giant staircase. He came to a stop at the river bank, staring at the moonlit water. It was deep and fast-flowing : he doubted that Cabra or Teresa would chance swimming across. He began to run in the direction of the bridge.

When he reached the wooden structure he halted again, breathing heavily. It was impossible to tell how much of a start his quarry had on him, but he guessed that with first two women and now only the one, it couldn't be too much. He loped over the planking, moccasins slapping on the boards, and entered the town.

The moon cast the only light as he moved past the shacks and warehouses that formed the southern outskirts, then slowed as he came into the town proper. He had no way of telling where the money Linda had talked about was stashed, or even if that had been merely a ruse. Probably not, he decided; a man like Cabra – and a woman like Linda – seemed the kind to set up some sort of insurance. But where? If it was in a bank, they'd have to get someone to open the place. If it was in a house – the *alcalde*'s place, maybe – they'd have to explain to whoever remained there. One thing he felt certain of : they wouldn't stick around Santa Rosa. Not with Vickers' men up in the convent. So : they'd want horses.

He came into the central plaza and edged into the shadow of a cantina. The statue of the nun at the centre shone white in the moon's light, shadow pooling around the basin of the fountain. The bank was silent; dark. Aranjuez's house looked deserted, but that could have been simply the blanking effect of the shutters covering the windows. He thought about trying the place. Decided against it : there could still be *pistoleros* in there, more than he could handle.

Instead, he turned for the stable.

The place was dark as the rest of Santa Rosa, the high, double doors padlocked shut. He tested the small, man-sized door at the side : it was open. He moved in, the Colt in his hand. The stable smelled of fresh hay and horses. One snickered softly as he came inside, shifting in its stall to follow him with gently curious eyes. He checked the stalls, drifting cat-silent from one to another. There were twelve ponies stabled and four empty bays. Each one was clean, showing no sign of droppings that might have indicated a recent departure. Cabra and Teresa were, he decided, still in town.

He went out of the stable and positioned himself on the sidewalk facing the doors. A porch slanted over his head, blocking out the moon so that he stood in deep shadow. He waited.

The moon moved slowly across the sky. Somewhere up on the ridge a dog barked. Another answered it, and then there was silence again.

Then the silence was broken by a single gunshot. Azul spun round, peering across the plaza in the direction of the sound. It had been muffled, but it seemed to come from the *alcalde*'s house. There was a second, then three more. He tensed, waiting for the next move.

A door opened on an unlit room. Two dark shapes stepped onto the porch fronting the Aranjuez place and paused. Azul recognised the faint scratching of shells dropping into chambers and flattened against the wall. Moon's light glistened off a silvery-polished handgun, then briefly from an ivory butt. The shapes climbed off the porch and walked fast across the plaza. Both were tall and dressed all in black.

As they reached the centre, the halfbreed recognised Jose Cabra. Teresa was beside him, clutching up the skirts of her habit to keep pace with the Mexican's long strides. The bandit had a sack slung over his shoulder.

Their voices carried clearly in the early morning stillness.

'Why did you kill them?'

'They'd have wanted a share.'

'They might have helped us. We could have started up again.'

'We shall. Somewhere else they trust nuns.'

'Suppose those men come after us?'

'How? Who knows where we've gone?'

'They might.'

A laugh; cold and cynical. Then, 'I'll kill a priest. Take his vestments. Who'll question a priest and a nun?'

'I would.' Azul stepped off the porch into the moonlight. The Colt was in his hand. Cocked. Pointed at Cabra's midriff. 'Drop the sack.'

Teresa gasped, one hand flying to her mouth in a curiously feminine gesture. Cabra just grunted a curse and let the sack fall from his shoulder. It clinked as it hit the ground.

'How did you find us?' His voice stayed calm.

'I spoke to one of your men,' said Azul. 'He leant me his ear.'

'The tunnel.' Teresa's voice was frightened. 'He must have found Linda.'

'The biggest hole she's ever been in,' acknowledged the halfbreed. 'I thought you two were friends.'

He set an obscene emphasis on the last word.

Cabra chuckled. 'Not where money is concerned, *amigo*. The lady loves gold. And I have plenty. Enough for three of us.'

He turned slightly as he spoke, indicating the sack at his feet.

'I'm going to kill you,' said Azul. 'For what you did to me.'

'Is that why you brought those *gringos*?' Cabra shrugged. 'Who were they, anyway?'

'Army,' rasped Azul. 'From over the Border.'

'I thought that.' Cabra nodded. 'Just because of what I did?'

'Yeah.' Azul smiled, though no humour showed on his face. 'I needed men.'

'I admire you.' Cabra's teeth showed white. 'I could use a man like you.'

He gestured again at the sack, turning to kick it.

'There's a lot of money in there, *amigo*. Join us.'

As the sentence ended he pivoted on his outflung foot, shifting his weight over in a single fast movement that spun him round behind Teresa. His left arm circled the woman's waist, pinning her hands to her sides. His right snatched the silver Colt from the holster, thumbing the hammer back and triggering a shot at the halfbreed.

Azul powered to the side. He couldn't tell why he didn't fire. Maybe it was because he remembered Teresa saving his life. Maybe it was because he remembered her body. Naked at the river; pressed against him after the Yaqui attack. Whatever the reason, he held the hammer of his own gun back and rolled over the porch with Cabra's bullets chasing splinters from the wood behind him.

He tumbled off the end and came to his feet behind the sheltering edge of the building.

Cabra laughed. 'You are soft, *amigo*. I'd have shot through her.'

'Maybe I want to see your face when you die,' Azul called back. 'In the open. Not hidden behind a woman.'

'You won't.' Cabra's voice got cold. 'I'm going out of here with her. Unless you want to see her die, you throw your gun out. The belt, too.'

He switched the angle of his gun, pressing the muzzle up against Teresa's cheek.

'For God's sake!' The woman's voice climbed high as fear overtook her. 'He means it! Please do what he says.'

'She's right,' said Cabra. 'I'll kill her and take my chance with you.'

'I saved you,' added Teresa. 'I saved your life twice. Back in Ysabel, then when Linda wanted to kill you. Please! José will let you go.'

'Sure,' said the Mexican. 'Just throw the belt over.'

Azul stared at them. Black on black. The silver of Cabra's gun barrel against the honey colour of the woman's face. Her lovely eyes were very wide; pleading. Her full lips were parted. He wondered what had happened that night he was drunk. Then, slowly, he dropped the Colt's hammer and slid the pistol into the holster. He reached down to unfasten the thong from his thigh. Began to unbuckle the belt.

'Well?' Cabra demanded.

Azul hefted the belt in his right hand. Cabra had fired four times, so he only had – at best – two shots left. Maybe just one, if he loaded on only five chambers. Would he chance using up his last shots if he thought he could make his getaway unhindered?

The halfbreed tossed the belt out into the plaza. It flailed through the cool night air. Thudded to the ground at the Mexican's feet.

'That's good, *amigo*. That's very sensible. I might even let you live.'

Cabra stooped, forcing Teresa down with him, and draped the belt over his left shoulder. Then he stepped back, dragging the woman. He muttered something Azul couldn't hear, and she lifted the sack. Her arms were still pinned by the Mexican's grip, so it was difficult for her to get a hold on the thing. She fumbled awkwardly at the neck, bending forwards so that for a moment her head obscured Cabra's vision.

It was just an instant, but that was all the time Azul needed.

He stooped to the side, right hand reaching down to fasten on the hilt of the throwing knife protruding from his moccasin. He palmed it and came upright again without Cabra spotting the sudden movement. His thumb pressed the slender, razor-edged length against his fingers, his hand hanging by his side.

'All right.' Cabra began to move across the plaza in a shuffle, keeping Teresa's body between him and Azul.

'You have sense, *amigo*. For that, I'll let you live. I like a man with sense. Now I want you to saddle our horses.'

He motioned with the Colt for Azul to step away from the shelter of the building. The halfbreed obeyed the gesture, noticing that the moon had shifted far enough over by now to fill the alleyway with a wan light.

'Stop there!' Cabra halted him at the centre of the alley. 'I'm crossing in front of you.'

He put the gun back against Teresa's face as he moved sideways towards the stable door. When he reached it, he paused, driving his right elbow back to slam the panel open. The woman still shielded his body, but the movement caused him to lean slightly to the side, his face shifting fully clear of her's.

And Azul moved.

It was very fast. Swift as a diamondback's strike.

And just as deadly.

The halfbreed brought his right arm up above his head. Then down in a single flow of swift movement, his fingers opening as the arc reached a horizontal plane.

The throwing knife glittered briefly, then was lost as it pierced Cabra's right cheek. It dug into the flesh between cheekbone and jaw, the force of Azul's throw driving it back through the muscle at the rear of the throat, slicing the root of the tongue. Cabra gagged, spitting blood. The Colt exploded a bullet in Azul's direction, but the halfbreed wasn't standing anymore. Instead, he was hurling forwards, straight at the bandit.

Teresa screamed and tore herself free of Cabra's loosened grip. The Mexican ignored her as he triggered a second shot over Azul's head. The knife was still jutting from his mouth and blood was drenching his shirt as he ground his teeth together, slicing the blade against his gums and lips. Azul hit him at full run, shoulder slamming into his chest so that Cabra was driven backwards, his boots catching on the raised sill of the door. He pitched full length, Azul landing on top of him, inside the stable.

The horses stamped nervously, starting to whinny as

the two men engaged in a lethal struggle that both knew must end in death.

Cabra ignored the knife jutting from his face as he pounded the empty Colt against Azul's head and shoulders. The halfbreed ignored the blows, reaching up to grasp the hilt of the knife and twist it free of the Mexican's jaw. The blade was slick with crimson as it came out, tearing an inches-wide gash in the side of Cabra's face so that his mouth was hugely enlarged, like a weird, death'shead grin. He dropped the Colt, fastening both hands on Azul's wrist as the halfbreed sought to drive the blade down into his throat. They rolled, desperation lending the bandit unnatural strength. He forced Azul's hand away, ramming a knee upwards in a vicious blow that would have crippled his opponent had it landed. Instead, Azul sensed it coming, twisting his body so that it struck on his thigh. Even so, the force was sufficient that pain lanced through his leg, already wearied by the run from the mountain. And Cabra took the opportunity to lurch away. He let go of Azul's wrist with one hand, smashing a fist against the halfbreed's chin.

Azul felt his teeth snap shut and lifted his forearm to counter the next blow. Cabra grunted, dripping blood over Azul's face, and lifted to his knees. He straddled the halfbreed, still clutching the knifehand, and stretched clawed fingers towards Azul's eyes. With the strange clarity that comes on the flow of danger-induced adrenalin through the body, Azul saw that the hand was oddly delicate, the nails long and sharp, dirtied by the escape through the caves. He turned his face to the side. Cabra's hand fastened in his shoulder-length hair and the bandit began to pound his head against the floor of the stable. Azul reached up for Cabra's throat. The Mexican jerked his head away, turning it to the side so that instead of his windpipe, Azul's hand fastened on the flap of skin hanging loose from his jaw. The halfbreed tore it down and out, extending the slit and ripping the fold clear of the lower angle of bone. Cabra's teeth showed a blood-stained white as the soft flesh of his lower gums was exposed. He screamed, his body tensing with the pain. Azul arched his back, humping the bandit over on his side.

Cabra's eyes were watered with agony as the halfbreed went on tugging at the fold of skin, like a man stripping a chicken. He let go of Azul's hair. Let go of his wrist. And clamped both hands about Azul's in an attempt to end the skinning of his face.

Azul thrust the knife up and over, driving the blade into Cabra's side, just above the belt. The Mexican grunted, not yet feeling the stab. Then Azul yanked the blade clear and something like a kick seemed to jerk Cabra rigid. He twisted sideways, as though seeking to avoid the pain, and rolled onto his back. Azul let go the flap of loose skin and slammed his hand, open-palmed against Cabra's jawline. It came away crimsoned as he lifted up to plant his knees on the bandit's arms. His left hand came down to fasten on Cabra's throat, and his right held the point of the knife close to the Mexican's eyes.

Cabra stared at him, a mixture of defiance and terror and rage mingling on his once-handsome features.

'I told you I wanted to see your face,' grated Azul. 'When you die.'

He drove the throwing knife down into the right eye. It sliced the orb, turning the pupil a milky white that was suddenly reddened as blood flowed from the edges of the socket. It drove on into the brain and the halfbreed put all his strength against the hilt, forcing it on and down until the tip struck the bone at the rear of Cabra's skull and pierced through. It dug into the earth covering the stable's floor, pinning the bandit like some gigantic insect in a collector's display. Nervous shock funnelled through his body. A scream erupted from his ruined mouth. His spine arched, bootheels drumming madly against the packed dirt. Azul was flung clear, fetching up on hands and knees as Cabra writhed, his hands gouging channels that filled with blood as his nails broke and tore loose.

The halfbreed watched him die, his face impassive with cold satisfaction.

After a while the writhing stopped. The nervous tremors slowed and ceased. One final ghastly rattle bubbled from Cabra's mouth, and he was still. Azul dragged the knife clear of the skull and wiped the blade clean on the dead man's shirt. Then he stood up, sheathing the weapon back inside his moccasin. He picked up his gunbelt and fastened it around his waist. There was a water trough ready-filled in an empty stall where he sluiced Cabra's blood from his face and hands. Then he went outside.

Teresa was standing facing a bunch of Mexicans. Some held guns, others machetes or knives.

'I told them it was between you,' she said. 'That Jose killed the men in Aranjuez's house. That they mustn't harm you.'

Azul looked at the watching faces.

'What did they say?'

'That they'd abide by my decision. They've always done what the Sisters told them.'

'And your decision?' he asked.

Instead of answering, she turned back to the townsfolk. 'Go home. Don't touch him. There will be more men coming through soon. Let them. Don't attack them. It's all finished.'

The crowd drifted slowly away into the grey mist of the dawn. Over to the east the sky was getting light. A rooster began to crow. Teresa tugged the headpiece loose, her hair falling in thick folds around her face. She fumbled with the fastenings of the black habit, shucking it away from her shoulders so that it fell about her feet in a puddle of darkness. Underneath, she was wearing a divided skirt; a short-waisted riding jacket. She looked very lovely.

'What will you do with me?' she asked.

Azul shrugged. 'Let you go, I guess.'

Surprise registered on her face, disbelief slowly giving way to hope.

'You came all this way, and now you'll let me go?'

'You saved my life,' he replied. 'I've got what I wanted.'

'Those soldiers will take me back.' She looked southwards, up the ridge to where a fiercer glow than the dawnlight lit the misty sky. 'They'll take me for trial in America.'

'They can't,' said Azul. 'If you're not here.'

She looked at him curiously, then, 'There's a key just inside the stable.'

He nodded, stepping back through the door. The key was hanging on a nail. He took it down and opened the padlock. Swung the doors open. Flies were clustering over Cabra's body and a busy line of beetles was marching steadfastly towards the corpse. He stepped over it and led a bay gelding out from a stall. There was a saddle nearby that would fit her: he put it on the horse.

'I guess they owe you, too.' He gestured at the town. 'You helped make them rich enough.'

'You're a strange man.' Her voice was wistful. 'I wish I'd known you before.'

'Before what?' Azul grinned. 'Before you were a nun?'

She smiled. Then stepped close to him. Her eyes were almost level with his. Her arms went around his neck and her eyes closed as her lips parted. They were warm and soft, full of all kinds of promise. Her tongue thrust into his mouth and he felt her breasts against his chest, her stomach flat against his. Almost against his will he felt the longing he had known before stir inside him. He crushed her against his body.

Then pushed her away.

'You'd best get going.'

She looked at him for a long moment, her eyes smoky. 'Thank you,' she said at last. 'Maybe we'll meet again.'

'Maybe,' nodded the halfbreed.

She led the horse out of the stable, standing it in the alley as Azul swung the doors shut and returned the key to its place. When he came out again she was mounted.

'Where'll you head?' he asked.

'North,' she replied. 'I've had enough of Mexico.'

'Be careful.' He smiled at her. 'That can be a dangerous journey.'

She laughed and nodded. Then drove her heels against the bay's flanks and took it across the plaza at a canter. 'Thank you,' she called. 'For everything.' And was gone into the mist lifting up from the river.

Azul listened until the hoofbeats had died away, then turned to where she had dropped the sack. It wasn't there anymore.

He began to laugh.

Vickers and his men reached Santa Rosa late in the afternoon. They were bringing three wagons, one carrying the remaining women. They found Azul slouched at a table outside a cantina, drinking tequila.

'What happened?' asked the major. 'You catch up with them?'

Azul nodded, pointing across the plaza to where an old man was hammering nails into the lid of a coffin. It was a plain pine box, not decorated.

'Jose Cabra,' he said. 'He didn't have enough on him to pay for anything better.'

Vickers shrugged, helping himself to a drink.

'It's finished,' he said. 'We got everything we came for, and then some.'

'What about them?' Azul indicated the women climbing from the wagon.

'I'll leave them here.' Vickers chuckled. 'They got nothing left now. Best they can hope for is a bed in a whorehouse. Besides, we ain't supposed to be here.'

'No,' murmured Azul. 'I guess we start back.'

'You coming along?' Vickers sounded doubtful.

'I'm owed money,' grunted Azul. 'Remember? Seven-fifty, and Scout's Pay. Like you promised.'

Vickers nodded, reaching inside his shirt. He brought out a wad of notes and dropped them on the table. 'Seven hundred and eighty dollars. Way folks feel about you in Ysabel, it'd be best you don't go back.'

'Maybe.' Azul picked up the money. 'I guess the last visit got me into some bad habits.'

He rode with them as far as El Rio, then struck off to the west, heading up towards the New Mexico line. Towards the country he still thought of as home. Along the way he thought a lot about Teresa.

BETTER TIMES THAN THESE

BY WINSTON GROOM

The shattering classic novel of a dirty war

'Bravo' company, U.S. Seventh Cavalry. Raw recruits and
ambitious commanders. Men with the tradition of General
Custer and the Indian wars behind them. This is the story of
another bloody chapter in American history: the battle of
Ia Drang valley, and of the soldiers who fought there. But it is
more than the story of those soldiers: it tells of the world –
and the women – they left behind them, and of what happened
when they came up against the horrors of combat. It shocks,
horrifies, moves and enthralls – because it always tells the
raw truth.

'A mirror of hell that leaves one awestruck'
NEW YORK TIMES

'A thoroughly realistic portrait of men at war . . . frightening
. . . genuinely merits comparison with James Jones'
PUBLISHERS WEEKLY

WAR   0 7221 4100 9   £1.75

THE GRAIL WAR

BY RICHARD MONACO

THE SOARING MEDIEVAL FANTASY

'A tall knight whirled an axe stroke at Parsival, who leaned slightly away, and the blow chugged into a tree and stuck. He didn't bother to return the compliment, just blocking and ducking, keeping his nervous horse moving through the frustrated, struggling mass of fighters . . . Another charged him and then the horse jammed between two trees . . . Another backed away from the thrust by Gawain and was unseated by a heavy limb . . . Smoke cut the battle into ghostly fragments . . . a man riding headless . . . a horse dancing on another . . . a bodiless arm swinging, clutching a branch . . . two knights wrestling in the blood-dewed brambles . . . men climbing over one another, the ones underneath creating a bridgeway over the prickly tangles, screaming . . .'

- THE GRAIL WAR

A magnificent, stirring and beautifully moving Arthurian tale in the classic fantasy tradition of LORD OF THE RINGS.

FANTASY   0 7221 6165 4   £1.75